CHALK TRACKS

Originally a Londoner, the Downlands stole Gina Challen's heart when she moved to West Sussex in 1979. Her passionate interest in rural life and the chalklands continues to inspire her writing.

She completed a Masters in Creative Writing at the University of Chichester in 2014. Her stories have appeared in numerous anthologies. Two were shortlisted for the Bridport Prize in 2014 and another was longlisted for the RSL's VS Pritchett Prize in 2018. *Chalk Tracks* is her debut collection.

Chalk Tracks

Stories from the Downlands

GINA CHALLEN

VP

Valley Press

First published in 2019 by Valley Press
Woodend, The Crescent, Scarborough, YO11 2PW
www.valleypressuk.com

ISBN 978-1-912436-22-4
Cat. no. VP0142

A CIP record for this book is available from the British Library.

Cover by Fitzpatrick Designs.
Text design by Jo Haywood.

Contents

for Leanne and Grant, with all my love

Up to Bignor

Magpie

HE FEELS AS if he has always lived here, tucked away in the fold of the Downs, with the bulk of the hillside behind him. To the south, farmland stretches across the coastal plain, wrapping itself around the towns and parishes before giving way to the sea. On a clear day, standing on the top of the hill, he can see the Isle of Wight. It shifts and shimmers in the light, as if it is floating out there on the distant horizon. But, when the cloud is low, mist rolls out across the fields, hiding the village under a thick, damp blanket.

He doesn't have a steady job. When he's needed, he labours on neighbouring farms. He works with the seasons, coppicing in winter, lambing in spring and harvesting in summer. He cleans ditches, cuts back hedgerows and keeps the footpaths open. In the autumn, he forages in the woods for cauliflower fungus. He carries a stick made from a twist of hazel. The wood at the top is smooth from years of handling and feels at home in his fingers. He uses the stick to poke around the base of pine trees, pushing back brambles to reveal the fungi. With a short-bladed knife, he cuts the branching stems and lifts the sweet, creamy mass.

When he works, he wears a brown jacket. It's old and discoloured. Stains spreading across the fabric like moss on the bark of a tree. If the weather is too hot for a coat, he carries a canvas game bag strung across his chest. He was christened Jacob, but, as a small boy, his granny called him Magpie.

The village is the only home he has known, but he wasn't born here, he's a *furriner*, brought across from Brighton as a baby. While he's growing up, he understands this makes a difference. Besides, he's heard the stories of his mother's disgrace and the gossip about her mini-skirted ways, the whispers of the adults repeated in the taunts of older children. *You're a come-by-chance, and y'mum's mawky. She's a slut, and that's no better than she should be.*

Each year, on his birthday, a card arrives in the post. He places it in an alcove of the fireplace, next to a china shepherdess. The picture of a carefree Mickey Mouse, with his red shorts and yellow shoes, stands out like a blemish against the dull brickwork. If he's lucky, he finds a fold of dollar bills caught in a paper clip and secured beneath the greeting. He keeps them, still folded, in a tin under his bed along with the envelopes the cards came in. After his sixteenth birthday, the cards stop arriving.

His mum is bound to come back for him when she's settled. His granny tells him this. Or perhaps she'll send for them both, and they'll have an adventure going across the sea to live with her. Try as he might, he can't imagine his granny ever leaving the village, but the year he's thirty-five and she's eighty-three, she leaves him. People said that she had made old bones.

He keeps the cottage the same as it has always been, coats hung on the pegs inside the back door, boots and bags jumbled in the corner and fungi in nets, dangling above the Aga to dry. His granny's clothes still hang in the wardrobe. Now he's alone, he likes to read. His favourite books are westerns, biographies and whodunits, which he buys at random from church fetes. There's something comforting in owning these fragments of other peoples' lives. Once a fortnight, he orders books from the library van. He reads about explorers and travellers, about nomads and gypsies, and about the pioneers who trailed across America in search of another place to settle. He learns of their treks, mile after mile. He learns of covered wagons pulled by mules, of deaths, of births, of hardship and joy. He memorises the facts. Most of all, he likes to read about people who have journeyed across rivers and mountains, searching for a different life.

Fridays, if he has cash, he drinks cider in the pub, leaning against the bar with his friends. He drinks his cider quickly, throwing back his head, his Adam's apple chasing up and down. The empty glass rocks as he sets it down waiting for another. He has grown up with these men, sitting next to them in school and working beside them on the land. Now they are older, they call him Mag.

They talk about football and the cost of the Olympics. They argue about culling badgers, trade stories about foot and mouth and worry about the threat of a new virus devastating the flocks. If the conversation turns to women, he finds a reason to down his pint and leaves.

These men no longer remember the belongings that went missing from their desks. Yet, Mags can still see them, young boys in the playground, yelling, *Magpie's a fucking spazz,* as they upturned his rucksack and spilled the hoard he had gathered across the ground. He has never forgotten the sudden pounding in his chest or how tears lurched from behind his eyes, while he stood, head bowed, in a shower of sweets, pencils and bits of loose change.

When he walks around the village, he finds things. He knows how to look. He retrieves old tickets and odd coins from the bus stop, a pen from the porch of the village hall and cigarette butts smudged with lipstick from outside the shop. Later, back at the cottage, he places them safely amongst his collections. Sometimes, while he waits in the farm office, he slides his hand into the pockets of unguarded coats, his fingers searching amongst creased tissues for hidden treasures.

In the lambing sheds, he takes the night watch, moving easily amongst the ewes, tugging newborns free and wiping mucus from their mouths. He clears the placentae into buckets for burning and sprinkles antiseptic powder across the fresh straw. It's warm inside, the air heavy with the breath of a hundred animals and the acrid smell of urine and blood. It's not unpleasant, but still he drinks his coffee outside in the clean, cold air, watching for the dawn.

There's a woman working in the shop who he speaks to. She's new to the village and there's talk about her in the pub. Where she has come from. Why she is here. She always smiles at him when he buys his paper. They chat together. They discuss the weather, television programmes, how to stop smoking and what they will cook for dinner. He likes the way she knots a scarf around her neck and how her hair shifts and shines under the lights as she moves behind the counter. He sees the tight fit of her jeans as she bends to stack the shelves. When he can, he helps her close the shop. He puts out the rubbish and breaks down the empty boxes. He sweeps the floor and waits while she cashes up the till to walk her home.

He talks to her about his work on the hillsides and about the books he is reading. One afternoon, he places a feather from the wing of a green woodpecker on the counter. He tells her how he found it outside the school. How he spotted it lying against the railings, amongst the dead leaves. Taking it up, she says, 'Funny, it looks yellow in the light.' And traces the colour with her fingertip.

'So pretty,' he says.

Then he tells her about the woods and how he looks for the cauliflower fungus.

'I found my stick leaning up against the wall in the porch of the church,' he says.

She looks up at him and says, 'Somebody must have lost it. I'm surprised they didn't come back, aren't you?'

He's puzzled by her question. 'I don't know. I wanted a good stick,' he says.

Later, when he helps her tidy up, she says, 'It must be fun, foraging.'

'We'll go in the autumn,' he says. And he puts his arm around her shoulders. She jerks away, telling him she will be much too busy to go.

'And I'm in a rush, tonight,' she says. 'I've got a date. A film, then dinner. Why don't you go, I can manage here. Really, I can. You go.' She looks straight into his face. He can see the rigid tendons in her neck, the gloss of her lipstick.

'Please, go.'

He stands for a moment, his hands on his thighs, his fingers splayed, as if he is holding himself upright.

'Please,' she says. He hears the catch of her voice in her throat.

As he lets himself out through the back door in the storeroom, he spots her scarf, draped across a chair. He lifts it to his face and brushes the cool, shiny material against his lips. He slips the scarf into his pocket.

He spends the end of summer mending fencing and stiles. His pickup is loaded with posts and planks and he travels across the farmland from site to site. The work is hard. He digs out rotten posts and beds in the new, pulling taut the strands of wire and securing them with metal staples to the wooden posts. He's paid a day rate. He keeps a tally in his notebook. Glatting Hanger – eight days. Pitchurst Copse – six days. He always adds an extra day.

They come in the early morning when he is working his way down through Left Hanger, repairing the fence between the fields and the edge of the forest. There are four joggers, all women, legs outlined in black Lycra and water bottles in their hands. He stands aside, amongst a tumble of bramble and faded cow parsley, to let them go by. The last runner has dark hair tied back from her face.

'Morning,' she says.

And he sees the swing of her hips, and the muscles in her thighs. His hands are hot inside his heavy, leather work gloves. As she runs past, she leaves a trace of scent, sweet like wild honeysuckle.

The next day, he leaves his fencing to search for signs of cauliflower fungi. It's early September and the mushrooms have only just begun to grow. He probes around the scrub beneath the pines, noting the position of the fruits for later. It doesn't occur to him that the joggers may return, and, as he goes back through the wood to his work, he's surprised by the dull beat of their running. He crouches down. Through the dried heads of cow parsley and old man's beard, he spies the joggers moving along the footpath. The dark-haired woman pauses, her feet still marking time on the spot. She gulps water from her bottle and he sees the pale, secret hollow under her arm. He waits, motionless in the undergrowth, until her footsteps are echoes on the chalk.

It takes him three weeks to finish this job, working along the fence line, chopping back the undergrowth. He continues through the weekends. Each morning, cutting and hammering his way down the footpath, he watches for the runners. As he works, he thinks of how, tomorrow, no matter what, he will speak to her. Conversations form, disperse and reform, creating an ever changing dialogue, until all the words they could use fill his head.

In the evenings, he finds he can no longer read. He drops the paperback on the floor by his chair, not caring about the drama played out in the pages. Library books remain unopened, stacked on the table. He thinks about the woman running through the woods, wonders how it would be if he took her to the pub for a drink. She would be dressed in jeans and a silky top. He calls her Claire. He imagines her hair shifting across her shoulders as she walks. He feels the tingles as it brushes across the back of his resting hand.

Come Monday, it will be time to move on to his next job. He lays awake, curled on his side, staring at the window. By six o'clock, although it's still dark, he parks his pickup at Toby's Stone. He begins to track back through the woods to Left Hanger, forcing the bracken and bramble aside with his stick. In the cold air, he catches the musk of a fox, harsh and oily, and the undergrowth stirs as he passes. The sun rises. He hunkers down beside a pine tree. In his old jacket, he is no more than a shadow on the ground. He thinks of the fungi, untouched beneath the scrub. If he cuts one today, it will be the first he has taken this autumn.

He waits, once more watching the dawn light flame across the sky, until the familiar thud of trainers draws him and he creeps, tree by tree, towards the footpath. When the women have passed, he emerges, tilting his head towards the breeze.

From his game bag, he lifts the cauliflower fungus and carries it to the sink. The fruit is young, still milky white, the fragrance not yet matured. He should have left it to grow bigger, should have let it carry on thrusting out lobes and collecting up the minute debris of the forest floor. He holds it under the tap, letting the running water rinse out a hoard of grit and pine needles.

Tonight, he will fry the fungus and make an omelette. He cracks three eggs into a bowl and beats them with a fork, piercing the membrane around the yolks and whisking until the liquid froths a deep, pure yellow. With a twist of his wrist, he glides a knob of butter across the hot surface of the frying pan. While the butter melts, he takes a sharp knife and cuts through the flesh of the fungus, sliding the slices back into the sink. He uses his fingers to feel for any remaining cache of dirt.

When he touches a hard swelling deep within the lobes, he thinks he has found a small stone buried in the soft fungal tissue. If he's right, he will keep the stone in a box with others he has found. As if he were shelling a bean, he draws his thumbnail across the top and hooks the object free. An earring falls out, coming to rest in his hand. Against his palm, three red gems set in a gold mount glisten like sparks from a fire. He lets the earring fall onto the table, stepping back as if he were in danger of being burnt. On the Aga, the searing butter hisses and spits in the pan. As it browns, it fills the kitchen with the bitter aroma of charred cob nuts.

He sits at the table, drinking coffee, looking at the earring. He rolls it between his thumb and forefinger, feeling the rise of the gold against the faceted gems. He closes his fist around it and, holding it tight, reaches for a library book. He reads of Native Americans, Blackfoot, Apache and Sioux, riding their horses across wide open plains. He reads the stories of these hunters and gatherers, of necklaces made from carved stones and of the willow hoop of the dream-catcher, decorated by the shaman with the findings of everyday life.

As the dark begins to fade, he wraps the earring in a cotton handkerchief he has taken from his granny's room and places it in the pocket of his jacket. He drives to Left Hanger and leaves his pickup in a gateway. On foot, he follows the hedge line to where the footpath curves into the woods. Shielded amongst the hawthorn, he waits.

~

'Have you lost anything?' He steps forward as the first woman climbs the stile. Today her dark hair lies in a plait across her shoulder. There is a slight sheen of sweat across her forehead.

'Jesus Christ. I didn't see you.' Behind her, the other women are jogging on the spot, their breath ragged in the cool morning air.

'I found this.' He takes the handkerchief from his pocket and uncovers the earring. His palm outstretched, he offers it to her.

'Oh.' She lets go of the upright post and moves away from him. He sees her teeth bite against her bottom lip. 'It's not mine.'

'It's for you. Please, take it.' He smiles.

Without turning away from him, the woman stretches back with her foot and manoeuvres herself onto the stile.

'Come over this side with us,' her friend says, reaching out to guide her. 'She's never seen it before, alright.'

The women edge away, pace by pace, until, as one, they begin to run. Again, the morning is filled with the beat of their steps along the path. His fist closes tight around the earring until he can feel the edges, sharp against the flesh of his palm.

'Claire?' he says.

Fair Game

THE SCREAM RIPPED across the night, tearing her from sleep. She knelt on the bed, jerked open the curtains and stared out of the window. Bit by bit, shapes emerged from the stillness until Robyn could make out the straight lines of the post and rail fencing, the confused mass of distant trees and, to one side, the old hawthorn hedge.

It was cold in her room, the chill cut across her bare arms. She gave a last glance outside and caught a fluid movement along the bottom of the hedgerow. Now, with the quilt wrapped around her shoulders, she waited for the form to materialise. At first, there was a flash of white, a tease, then another, but before she could make out its outline it was gone, lost within the shadows.

Her body was warm in its covering and as she leant against the glass, resting her cheek on the wooden frame, she heard the heavy throb of a diesel engine struggling up the hill. She moved back from the window and, shielded by the curtains, watched the headlights sweep round the corner, bringing the fence line to life. Once more, she caught a blaze of white, then the gleam of eyes, green in the sudden brightness. Uncertain, she thought there was the dark, limp shape of a kill in the animal's mouth. Before she could be sure, the pickup drove past and the fox was gone.

On waking, her first thought was of the fox, the way it tilted its head as if to look at her, the way it was trapped for a moment in the beam of the headlights. She wondered if she would see it again. When her mum called her, she didn't answer. What was the point in answering her anymore? She dressed in a short black skirt, thick black tights and a sheer, white blouse. In the mirror, her face was painted pale, her lips a deep bruised plum and her eyes marked round in heavy, black liner. Before leaving the room, she pushed her feet into spike-heeled shoes, shrugged on a denim jacket and grabbed her bag.

In the kitchen, her mum was staring out of the window, a mug of coffee in her hands. These days, her mum was quieter. She laughed less often. Even her clothes seemed muted in shades of grey or brown.

'Are you eating, Robyn?' her mum said. 'Cereal? Toast?'

'Not hungry,' she said, waiting for an argument. Waiting for her mum's voice to rise in concerned anger. But there was no reply. Nothing. There was only silence. Robyn wondered if she should mention the fox and tell how its cries had woken her, or perhaps talk about seeing the kill in its mouth.

Her mum turned from the window. 'I'm not saying anything else after this. What can I do?' She shrugged. 'You're fifteen. You look ridiculous. You're angry. God knows, that's plain enough.' She paused. Robyn looked at her mum but didn't answer.

'It's difficult for you, Robyn. For us. But you're hurting yourself. Nothing will change. And, honestly, I'm tired of it all. You want to carry on like this, fine. I'm not arguing anymore. Let me know when you decide it's over.' And putting the mug on the draining board, her mother walked out of the room without another word.

Robyn sat at the back of the classroom, elbows planted on the desk, running her fingernail along the vane of a feather to make the colours flicker. That morning as she was leaving home, she had seen it caught at the bottom of the hedge, the stripes of brown and cream bold against the green leaves of the brambles. She glanced around the room. Look at them all, she was surrounded by a class full of losers. Nothing was as boring as this crap. At her old school, even double Spanish had been better than anything this dump had to offer. And no one could be bothered to mention her makeup. Or her clothes. All there was in this place were miles of grubby, grey corridors, echoing stairwells and roving packs of morons. Anyway, she had better stuff to think about. She had Jonnie.

There was Jonnie clearing out the ditch by the village green. Or with a chainsaw in his hands, cutting back the holly by the churchyard. Jonnie when he took a break, leaning against the bonnet of his pickup, teasing her, calling her his little shadow. And there was last Saturday, when he delivered a truck full of logs for her mum: his straight-legged jeans ripped at the knee, his t-shirt a well-worn blue and his work boots scuffed and muddy. She pictured the muscles in his arms as he stacked the wood, his easy grin when he told her he drank at The George and the coarse red hairs she had glimpsed at the nape of his neck. All through the lesson, little scenes of them together played out in her head.

When the bell rang, she hurried through the school to the sports arena, her bag bouncing heavily against her back. At least she hadn't been forced to give up athletics when she came here and, for what it was worth, she'd made the track team. The changing room was empty. Coats hung from pegs, bags clogged the benches and shoes littered the floor. Before undressing, she cleaned the makeup from her face, throwing the wipes into the bin, where they lay amongst the crumpled paper towels. She dumped her clothes in a locker, changed into leggings and a sweatshirt, and looped the earphones to her iPod around her neck.

The afternoon breeze was cold when she jogged across the field. From the hockey pitch, she could hear the shouts of the players and the whack of a ball against a stick. She put her iPod on shuffle and began her warm up stretches listening to '80s rock. This was her dad's music. Tears caught in the back of her throat. What was he doing right now? Whenever she listened to old songs she thought about him driving her to school, with the radio on, and the two of them laughing, singing to the music as loud as they could. It was simple, he wasn't around anymore. She never knew where he was these days, didn't know what clothes he was wearing, couldn't picture him at work. She could phone him, of course, but it wasn't the same. She began to run, her breathing steadying as she settled into a rhythm and the notes sweeping through her until they were pounded away with her steps.

She reached her last lap and, tugging her earphones free, jogged towards the buildings. Inside, it was quiet. The changing room held the remains of a floral scent trapped in the damp air and a line of smudged footprints led across the tiled floor.

~

Sitting on the bus, she took the feather from her pocket and once more ran her fingernail along the vane. As the bus rounded the corner, she could see the road outside their house was empty. Perhaps her mum was working late again. She dumped her bag in the hall and checked to see if there was a note on the pad by the phone, but there was nothing for her, only *Jonnie – Logs* written in black biro alongside a number. She entered the number into her mobile. Without turning on the lights, she walked up the stairs to her room, dragging the feather along the wall.

~

Although it was only six o'clock, his truck was in the car park. She wiped her finger across the scratched paintwork of the driver's door, tracing a heart in the dirt. He was in the pub. She could see him through the window, sitting on a stool, a pint by his elbow, talking to the landlord. It wouldn't be long before he came out to smoke. Her phone vibrated. Was it him? No doubt he had seen her and wanted her to go in. *Mum.* She cut the call. The wind was biting. She tucked in beside the wall, wrapped her arms around her chest, and waited.

The door opened and there he was: Jonnie. The glow from the bar catching red flecks in his hair as he bent his head to light a cigarette. When the match flamed, she saw stubble on his cheeks. Goosebumps raced across her arms. All she need do was move forward and she could stroke her fingers down his face. She stepped towards him.

'Alright?' he asked. 'What, you meeting someone?' He half turned to open the door for her.

'I saw a fox last night,' she said. 'I heard him calling.' Her breath hung in the evening air.

'That'd be a she-fox screaming, not a him. Calling for a mate. But I 'spect you didn't see her, you saw the old dog-fox on his way home.'

She opened her jacket and took the feather from the pocket of her shirt.

'I think it's a pheasant.'

'It is. Wing feather. Coming in?'

She shook her head. He flicked his cigarette away and it spun to the ground, releasing a thin coil of smoke when it hit the gravel. As soon as he had gone inside, she rescued the butt and knocked out the dying end against the ground. She brushed the warm filter across her lips. It left a bitter residue, like burnt caramel, on her mouth. It was as if she had tasted a tiny part of him. She slipped it into her pocket beside the feather.

When she saw him leave the pub, cloud was building and chasing across the moon.

'Hi, Jonnie.'

'Christ, you're still here. Must be bloody freezing,' he said, laughing. 'I'd better give you a lift home then, hadn't I?'

Her skirt rode up her thighs as she climbed into the pickup and she saw him staring at her legs. She tried to tug the hem down. He reached across her to wipe the windscreen and his arm brushed across her breasts. It was probably an accident. Her breath caught in the back of her throat. Now he would kiss her and it would be soft and delicate, full of love. But he sat back and gave her a quick wink before turning the key in the ignition. He's waiting, she thought, for the right moment.

He drove through the village and up the hill, leaving behind the rows of cottages and the families eating their meals, putting children to bed and settling down for the evening. She wished this time would last forever, the two of them being carried along in the warm cab, with the smoke from Jonnie's cigarette curling round them.

'Your mum not home then?' he said, stopping outside her house.

'No. You can come in, if you want. Have a drink or something.'

'Nah, don't think so. Maybe I'll look for that fox you saw.'

'I could go with you. Show you where he went. Please.' She glanced at the house. The curtains had been drawn and the light from the porch shone across two empty flower pots standing each side of the cracked step. The front door needed painting. No way was this house fine, whatever her mum said. Or quaint, which, however you looked at it, meant small, too small, definitely not big enough for them.

'You can't look for foxes dressed like this.' he said, drawing his thumb up her thigh and stopping at the edge of her skirt. His rough skin snagged against her tights. She swayed towards him.

'I'll change. I'll be really quick.' She put her hand on his sleeve. 'I promise.'

'Okay. Two minutes.' He pulled his phone from his pocket and began to check his messages.

Indoors, she snatched her leggings and trainers from her bag. Fumbling with the zip on her skirt, she read the note on the pad: *7.30 going shopping. Will get one of the pizzas you like for supper. Tried to call you. Please start your homework. Love Mum xx.* Like she said, she would be quick, quick, quick. Skirt off. Leggings on. Trainers on. No way would she make Jonnie cross because he was waiting around for her. She hoped he would spot how good her legs looked outlined by the Lycra.

'I nearly went without you.' He grinned and helped her onto the seat, running his fingertips across her knee as he reached for the gear stick.

She had never been so happy. They were a couple, going out together. In the half-light of the cab, she saw how he kept glancing at her. She was sure he was happy too. They left the road, the truck climbing up the hill on an old farm track. Perhaps, tomorrow, she could talk about him as *my boyfriend.*

Without warning, he veered the pickup sideways, leaving the track and bouncing across the rutted ground. She screamed and put her hand on the dashboard to steady herself. Tree trunks loomed out of the night, monsters bought to life in the jumping headlights.

'Slow down, Jonnie. Please. I don't like it.'

She felt the truck speed up. He laughed and squeezed her thigh.

'Please, we'll crash,' she said. Glancing at him, she saw he was grinning.

He winked at her. The headlights went off. Robyn screamed. He slammed on the brakes. The force jerked her forward, jarring her wrist. She fell back, the seatbelt pressing her against the torn leather of the seat. Had they hit something? Next to her, his voice loud in the darkness, he said, 'Don't worry I'll rub it better for you.' His hand closed around her breast.

His other hand still gripped her thigh, his fingers digging into her flesh. He lent across her and his mouth was on hers. There was a sour yeastiness on his breath. She couldn't breathe. She felt the hard edge of his teeth behind his lips. His tongue invaded her mouth. His fingers were scratching at her blouse, grabbing at the buttons. He lifted his head.

'This is more fun than looking for a fox,' he said.

'You're hurting me.' She put her hands against his chest to hold him away.

He reached up and cupped her face, his fingertips brushing the taste of stale nicotine across her lips. 'Is that better?' he said.

It would be alright now. She was being silly: Jonnie didn't mean to scare her. Robyn smiled and touched the back of his hand.

'I'm not hurting now, am I?' With his other hand, he undid the first button on her blouse. He caught hold of her hand and placed it on his crotch. His jeans were tight, the material warm. She felt the ridge of him against her palm.

'No, Jonnie.' She snatched her hand away.

'Look at me,' he said, gripping her chin between his finger and thumb. His face was close. 'What the fuck is your problem?'

'I don't – '

'You don't what?'

'I never – '

'Jesus, lighten up. Going a bit fast for you, am I?'

Once more, his lips covered hers. His hand scrabbled at her waist and crawled under her blouse. She gasped at the burn of his palm on her skin.

'That's good.' His voice was a low mumble. 'I need you to – ' taking her hand, he rubbed it against his crotch. 'Like that. You do it.'

She tried to move away from him, but the back of the seat trapped her in place.

'Undo them,' he said. And when she didn't, he sat back, fumbled the zip of his fly down and placed her hand in his open jeans.

'Please stop, you're scaring me.' Again, she shoved against his chest. 'I want to go home. Please, Jonnie. Mum will be back now. She'll be wondering about me.'

He didn't move. She shoved again. 'Mum, she'll be phoning me. Want to know where I am.'

'Christ,' he said. 'Listen to you.' He knocked her hands away. 'What are you? A kid? My mum will be back now. For fuck's sake, how old are you?'

'I'm sixteen. Soon. I'll be sixteen soon.'

'You stupid little bitch. Fifteen.' He slumped back against the seat. 'So you're nothing but another prick-teaser. Following me around. Flashing your legs. All wide eyes and tits on show.' She felt his movements beside her, the jut of his elbow and the scuffle of his feet on the floor. 'Come in for a drink, Jonnie.' His lighter flashed. 'Let me come with you, Jonnie.' She heard the intake of his breath. 'Don't tell me you weren't up for it. Fair. Fucking. Game. That's what you are.' With a sudden lunge, he was across her again. This time he opened the door. 'I'm done.'

'Jonnie?'

'Get out.' He pushed on her shoulder. 'Playing games are we?

Well, let's see how you like this game.'

He pushed her again. Harder. 'Out.' Overbalanced, she fell to the ground.

She heard the slam of the door. She heard the truck start up and the crunch of tyres against the stony ground. Robyn covered her face with her hands and lay on the hard mud, listening to the receding beat of the engine. The moon was covered by cloud and she was alone, lying in the open, feeling the cold seep through the knees of her leggings.

He would come back in a minute, she was sure. No way would he leave her like this. She sat up. As she adjusted to the darkness, she could make out the shape of a fallen tree and the bone-white mass of its root ball. She crawled towards it, dragging herself upright, the roots rough against her palms. Small stones scattered around her feet. But he was so angry with her. She wiped her hands on her legs and felt the weight of the mobile in her pocket. She pressed the buttons. The screen lit up and she scrolled through her contacts until a small, round picture of her mother's face smiled out at her. She drew her finger across the screen to connect the call. There was silence.

'Mum. Mum. Please. I need you,' she said, snatching the phone away from her ear. No signal. She stared out into the night and cried.

She rubbed her sleeve across her face. She was cold. With her hand on the root ball, she stepped forward, sliding her feet across the ground inch by inch until only her fingertips still touched the chalky soil. She sensed a movement behind her, a sigh as the dense scrub parted and a choking oiliness, pungent and repulsive, overwhelmed her for a moment. Grit trickled down against the back of her hand. She looked over her shoulder into the darkness. The sky cleared and there in the moonlight, standing on the fallen trunk, was a fox, its muzzle pointed towards her as it scented her on the wind.

It was him. Her fox. He had found her. When the animal jumped down, she followed his path, guided by the rustle of his passing through the undergrowth.

Clouds swept across the moon as the fox darted from the cover of the trees, out into an open field, trotting towards the copse on the other side. Once more the sky cleared, and there he was, his rust coloured coat flaming like a torch against the hard, brown earth. She hesitated, reluctant to leave the shelter of the wood. Half-way across, the fox stopped and she saw the blaze of his white throat as he looked back to where she was standing. She made up her mind, starting out after him along the ploughed furrows, her feet thudding on the frozen ground.

The fox began to lope, his movement graceful as he pressed forward. Then he was gone, lost from her sight in a tangle of brushwood. Behind her, she heard the raw pulse of a pickup. She could feel it, louder and closer, louder and closer, as if it was thumping to the beat of her heart. It must be him; what if he was still angry? She was caught, silhouetted in the headlights as they swept over the field. The engine screamed as the vehicle left the track.

Then she was amongst the trees, bending her face away from the thin branches that whipped across her body. Brambles snatched at her ankles, snagging her leggings. She mustn't fall. She ran deeper into the woods. It was quiet. She heard her own breath, ragged in her throat. Still moving forward, she wondered if he had left the pickup to follow her on foot. It could only be him, and she was certain he would be angry. Where was he? Robyn glanced back again and something cold and dank wrapped itself round her head.

She was blinded. Suffocated. She couldn't open her mouth to shout. She grabbed the covering, her nails clawing against it, her fingers slipping on the thick plastic. Jonnie. How had he got in front of her? How had he done this? Free, she must get free. She grabbed again, balling her hands into fists, ripping the plastic sheet from her face. He had her this time. Collapsing onto to the ground, she curled in the dead leaves, gulping in the trapped smell of fetid earth and the faint scent of the fox.

The night settled. She lay still. She could hear her own breathing and the distant hoot of an owl. Nobody spoke. Nobody touched her. She uncovered her face. Suspended above her, disembodied and dancing in the moonlight, was a line of empty feed sacks. Some hung from the trees, swaying back and forth, and others drooped from a wire fence. She stood. No sign of Jonnie. She placed her palm against the nearest sack. Polythene, slick with moisture. In front of her, enclosed by the fence, and empty at this time of year, was a group of wooden pheasant houses. Their roofs were rimed with an early frost and glistened in the clearing.

The bird pens. She had reached the bird pens.

The last time she had been here was the middle of June, before the poults were transferred to the release pens. So many birds scratching and pecking in the feed trays, with their quick, black eyes and the soft meld of cream and brown on their feathers. Her mum had held her hand and explained that, by Christmas, there would be a new sister for her. How wonderful it would be for Robyn. How her dad wouldn't love her any less now he was having another daughter. That she, her mum, loved her and – hugging her – that Robyn was her darling girl. And how, even though she missed him, she must be happy for her dad in his new life. She remembered the delicate strength of her mother's arms around her neck and the smell of her perfume.

When she checked, there was still no signal on her phone and she was surprised to find it was only half past nine. Taking care not to fall, she hurried from the enclosure and, following a footpath down along the old hedgerow, Robyn made her way home.

The night smelt of frost; crisp and clean. Part-way down, her mobile vibrated into life, the ring tone loud in the stillness. She snatched the phone from her pocket. She had a voicemail message from her mother and a list of missed calls. She clasped the phone in one hand. Leaving the path, she jogged along the road until the house came into sight. Again, she reached into her pocket, her fingers seeking the feather. But it had gone, falling to the ground unnoticed when she pulled out her phone. In front of her, a sliver of light escaped from around the edges of the sitting room curtains.

Before she could reach the gate, she heard the growl of an engine labouring up the hill. She shrank back into the hawthorn, until she could feel the thorns catching against her denim jacket. Headlights swung around the corner. Across the road, the front door opened and her mum stepped out. Robyn took a deep breath and darted across the tarmac into the garden. The truck drove past.

'Look at you. Where have you been? I was worried.' Closing her arms around Robyn, her mum watched the tail lights of the pick-up until they disappeared around the corner. 'Your hair smells of cigarettes. Please don't tell me you've started smoking.'

'I followed a fox,' Robyn said, allowing her mum to lead her to the house.

Before closing the door, Robyn looked back, noticing a fleeting movement along the bottom of the hedgerow. She waited to see the flash of a white throat or the gleam of an eye, but there was only movement, sleek and fluid. Then it was gone.

The Beekeeper's Daughters

I ARRIVE MID-MORNING, park on the gravel, grab the bouquet of flowers from the passenger seat and step out into a silence broken by bird calls. After living away, I forget it's so very quiet here: it catches me out every time I come back. The car leaves a city smell of hot metal and exhaust that clings in the air, harsh amongst the scents of wind blossom and dry, dusty undergrowth. All along the fence line, weeds and grasses are fighting their way upwards towards the light, and I hold my arms up, swaying away from the soaring nettles and purple-headed thistles.

There can be no doubt the view here is spectacular. Yellow rape and spiky, golden wheat are laid out across the landscape. Old woods, dark and mysterious, fill the secret creases between the rolling hills. I remember their names. Pitchurst Copse. Lamb Hanger. Scotcher's Bottom. Names that most people only see when they look on the ordnance map. Hazel, ash and beech. Oak, elm and holly. The trees are tightly tucked along the edges of the ancient pathways. I turn my back on the hills and look at the house. The cottage and garden appear to be tethered to the earth by a low flint wall, either side of which the wire fences stretch back into the distance, taut as guy ropes.

In the breeze, the wooden gate swings gently back and forth on the post, as if rocked by an unseen hand. The latch is lying, half-hidden, in the flowerbed. When I steady the gate, the blisters on the paintwork are ripe under my fingers, as ready to rupture as the fat flower buds on the bellbind creeping over the wall. Old Man's Nightcap, she calls it. I remember those summers, when we walked along the lanes and, stopping, make her pop the buds. It was as exciting as a magician's trick when we saw the milk-white blossoms burst free under the pressure of her fingers. The raw smell of sap would linger on her hands for the rest of the day.

On the garden path, loose paving stones rock under my feet. I'm surprised she hasn't slipped on them, ending up lying next to the latch, the pair of them rusting together amongst the weeds.

She hasn't come out to meet me, hasn't stood in the doorway, raking me with a look. Yet she knows I'm coming. Before I phoned her last week, I'd cancelled a dinner invitation, rearranged my weekend and booked the Monday off work. See you on Sunday, I said. Write it down. Then I called my sister to let her know when I'd be down at Mum's.

I find her at the bottom of the garden in the bee yard. I stand still and quiet in the gap between the lavender hedges to avoid being stung. She's lifted the lid from one of the hives and removed a super. They're heavy; I'm surprised she can still manage them. From here, it looks as if she holds a single living entity. Insects pulse against the mesh and the edges of the wooden frame are hazed by their beating wings. The bees cling together, shifting and changing position, like wisps of dark smoke. I can hear the low croon of her conversation and the steady hum of their reply.

Even in her beekeeper's suit, she looks smaller than last time I saw her, like a child who has raided the dressing-up box. She's shrunk in the last six months. The white jacket hangs in folds and her trousers sag at her knees. Her shoulders appear more rounded, as if she is hunched under the burden of her hat and veil. On her hands, she's wearing a pair of the pink rubber gloves she's favoured for years when tending the bees. On her feet, the slippers I sent her for Christmas.

My elbow aches from the weight of the flowers I'm holding, and the cellophane, wound tight around the stems, digs into my palm. I have no idea if she knows I'm here, but to avoid startling her, I edge slowly away. The back door is wide open. On the step, tucked to one side, sits a washing-up bowl full of windfall plums. They are bruised and split, and wasps have made wounds in the flesh. In the kitchen, I put the flowers on the table. I'm not sure if she owns a vase with sides tall enough for lilies.

Propped against the egg basket, where we have always left notes, is a message from my sister. She has been in with the shopping and made up my bed. Pick the peas, she says, and whatever else. I must take care not to leave the key in the back door when I go to bed. She'll be coming tomorrow about two. On the worktop, there's a small pile of vegetables, a few potatoes, two parsnips, some carrots. No doubt, my sister's counted them out. She hasn't changed. I can see her thinking there'll be enough for today, and fried up leftovers with the cold meat for Monday's lunch.

I could phone her, but I'm not sure what to say. It is not something we sisters do. I have never called her to chat, never called her to say, hi it's Lou, and how are you and the boys? Never listened while she talks about my nephews, and never shared my worries or asked her advice. We do not talk. The day I accepted my place at university, I had made my choice. I left. It is irreversible. I'm citified now. And that stands between us, as tangible as our mother's beehives.

I fill the kettle. Alongside the stainless steel canisters, the same thick china mugs still hang from the wooden mug tree. Red striped, orange striped and green striped, one for each of us. A residue of sour milk greets me when I open the door of the fridge, yet I can see my sister has wiped all the surfaces clean. There's very little in there. A joint of meat sits on the middle shelf beside a piece of vacuum-packed cheddar and a litre of supermarket milk stands in the door. The smell hangs around long after the fridge has been shut.

'What are you doing here?'

I feel my stomach clench. She's standing outside ready to step over the threshold and into the kitchen, and her hand, still in the rubber glove, is clutching the door frame. I didn't expect her at the house so soon and she's caught me checking my messages. I drop the phone into my pocket.

'Did you tell me you was coming?' she says.

'I phoned you, Mum. Last week. Thursday. Remember?'

She's staring at me and I know she's going to tell me I'm wearing too much makeup, my clothes are all wrong, trousers too tight, shoes too high, and my coat not practical. I focus on the grass stains across the toes of her slippers. Pieces of grit embellish the fur trim and they fall as she steps in, littering the floor, like some kind of cheap decoration she has sprinkled on herself.

'Didn't think I'd see you, eh? But I see'd you alright. What's she want, I thought to meself.'

She undoes her jacket and throws it to the floor, along with the hat and veil. She struggles with the cord on the trousers.

'Beekeeping clothes must be taken off outside. I thought that was the rule, Mum.'

'What do you know?'

I know I'm baiting her.

'In case you carry any strays indoors. That's what you've always told us.'

'Shut up,' she says, pulling the trousers off and sitting at the table. I don't answer, just watch as she peels off her gloves, turning them, finger by finger, the right way. Without looking at me, she grabs her mug and drinks the coffee I've made.

Later, we go down to the vegetable garden to pick peas. She moves with ease amongst the canes, seeking out the pods that are hidden in the leaves. Although her hands are thin and veined, they move across the stems as swift and sure as a wise woman casting a spell. Around us, the beds are a mess of dandelion, ragwort and self-set borage. Her bees slip in and out of the flowers, filching the pollen and storing it on their legs until, weighted down with yellow saddlebags, they fly back to the hives.

'That'll be poisonous,' she says.

'What?' I say.

'That's why she's gone and planted it here. The roots. Puts them in the tea,' she says, nodding her head at me. I look round to see what has caught her attention. I can hear a gentle patter as she drops the pea pods into the trug.

'Do you mean the ragwort?' I ask. 'Is that the problem?'

'You know,' she says, giving a short laugh. 'Told her to dig it out, but will she? The bees like it though.'

'Don't be silly, Mum,' I say. 'Jen didn't plant ragwort. Anyway, it's not poisonous to humans. You know that.'

She turns back to the pea canes.

'You too?' she says. 'Bitches the pair of you. In it together. I've got your measure.'

Then, all of a sudden, I've ceased to matter and her hands are busy once more, flitting amongst the plants, evoking their silent charms.

I am sitting on the step and Mum is on a kitchen chair with the silver colander on her lap. The trug is on the ground between us. The pods are empty and wilting, no longer heavy with the plump fullness of the peas. I dip my hand into the colander and let the smooth, cool peas, shift and roll through my fingers. I pop some in my mouth. She pats my arm and smiles at me. 'It's like you're choosing sweets from a bowl,' she says. 'Mind, you always did like them raw.'

The day smells of lamb roasting in the oven and mint chopped fine on a wooden board. The sharp tang of the broken leaves catches in my throat as I scrape them into a jug, ready to be mixed with sugar and vinegar.

After we've eaten, I leave her dozing in her armchair and start to clear away. In the back of the larder, lying on top of a box of empty glass jars, I find a metal milk pitcher. It is tall and elegant, and when I have dusted it off, the tarnished silver of the aluminium looks perfect with the milky white lilies. I stand it on the hearth, in front of the empty fire place, so she can see the flowers when she wakes.

'It'll stink in here by tomorrow, you mark my words. Funerals, that's where they belong,' she says.

Her voice is loud, startling me, and when I turn towards her, there is the glimpse of a smile, yet her eyes are still closed. I shut the door behind me as I leave.

In the garden, plums and apples lie rotting on the ground beneath the fruit trees and long stalks of wild fennel grow in the dishevelled grass around the trunks. Perhaps it is time to fetch a wheelbarrow and clear up all the fruit, or maybe find some shears and trim the edges of the lawn. Instead, I keep walking until I reach the gap between the lavender. It's peaceful in the bee yard. The lookouts dance in front of the hives, tirelessly beating their wings, flickering and spinning like tiny flaming beacons as they guide the wanderers home.

In the sitting room, the lilies have started to unfurl in the warmth of the day and fill the small space with a perfume as rich and heady as expensive wine. I kneel on the floor beside Mum's chair, turning the pages of a photo album. Here we are, Jen and me, grinning, gap-toothed, at a picnic. In another, a birthday party, there are balloons in the background, cake on the table and we are wearing matching party dresses, rose sprigged. My sister is smiling. I'm not. I hated that dress. Yet another photo and I'm brandishing an overlarge brush pretending to paint the beehives. Each event is annotated in our mum's spidery writing. My sister and me. Our childhood is fixed under cellophane.

'Look at them. My little girls. My Jenny and Louise,' she says, pointing to a picture.

I smile at the absurdity of us dressed up in her beekeeping clothes, my sister with the trousers gathered up under her arms, and me peering out through the veil.

'I don't remember that one, Mum. Nineteen seventy-seven, I was eight.'

She looks up at me and slams the front cover shut. I rock back, as if I've been slapped by the sudden noise.

'Where did you get this?' she says, holding the album fast against her chest. 'You'd better not have gone ferreting around. I'll know. Don't you be thinking I won't. Taking things. I've seen you. I'll call the police, I will. That'll put paid to you.'

Her face looks defiant and full of cunning, as if she has trapped me by her words. I feel off-balance. I feel that if I deny her accusations, by some strange logic, anything I say will only prove her right.

The creaking of the stairs wakes me. When I open the door, the light from my bedroom cuts a wedge through the night. From the landing, I watch her round the last step, wraithlike in her nightdress. Her hand is pale against the wooden newel post. Then she's lost to me in the darkness of the hall. The back door rattles, and I guess she's wrenching on the handle. I can hear her voice rising. Her words are disjointed, muddled as they travel through the space between us. The door rattles again. She shouts. I find my hands are clenched, my fingernails cutting into the flesh of my palms. Even from here, her frustration is palpable. It creeps towards me up the stairs and I back away from it into my room.

We stumble through the hours of the next morning. She appears in the kitchen dressed in her beekeeping suit. She's not talking to me, won't sit at the table, and doesn't want breakfast. I pour her a mug of tea. It's knocked away and the tea splashes across the table.

'Why must you be so bloody awkward?' My voice is loud.

I grab her arms and shake her. Beneath the sleeves of her jacket her bones feel bare. When I let go, she lets herself out of the back door and walks, with dignity, down the garden. I don't follow.

At lunchtime, I look for her. A strong smell of burning paper draws me towards the bee yard long before I spot the puffs of smoke. The smoker is lying, black-bellied, on the gravel, alongside her brushes, scrapers and a red Bic lighter. God knows how she got hold of a lighter. She glances at me and replaces the lid on a hive.

'Good honey,' she says, bending down to collect up her tools. 'There's plenty of it.'

'I'll carry them,' I say, nodding towards the ground.

'Thank you. Is it lunchtime?'

She hands me the smoker. When I reach to gather up the other equipment, the lighter has gone. Through the mesh of her veil, her smile is fragmented.

'Cold lamb. It's Monday. I'm hungry,' I say.

She puts her hand on my arm and we walk back to the house.

'You two always did like a nice bit of honeycomb,' she says.

My sister arrives as I'm serving the vegetables. She looks washed out. She is wearing a rust-brown blouse. It doesn't suit her. It's leached the colour from her face.

'You're early,' I say.

'Alright, Mum?' she says.

She doesn't look in my direction or ask how I am. Nice. In her usual way, my sister makes it plain she has no time for a family catch-up. I'm surprised to find that for once this bothers me, yet I'm glad I didn't phone her yesterday.

'Have you met my daughter?' Mum asks her politely, reaching for the mint sauce and spooning it over her plate. The specks of mint are vivid against the creamy fat on the meat and, as she eats, she mops up the vinegar with squares of fried potato.

Through the sitting room window, I watch my sister as she loads two suitcases into her car. I gather together the photograph album, a map of old Sussex I've taken from the wall, a radio and Mum's slippers. I pack them into a box. When I glance back outside, Jen is folding an eiderdown and squashing it on top of the cases. She closes the boot and the flowers on the material look as if they are being crushed against the glass. Good god, from where I'm standing the roses on the eiderdown remind me of that bloody party dress. I carry the box out.

'Ready?' my sister says.

'Are you sure about this?'

'That'll have to go on the back seat,' she says, grabbing the box from me.

'She's not that bad.'

'I've told you, she needs someone all the time,' she says, easing the box in the car.

She doesn't even turn to face me.

'Don't you ever listen?' she says.

'It'll kill her,' I say.

'What do you know? Two days you've been here, and you think you can sort everything out with a bunch of flowers – as usual.'

She still has the irritating rise to her voice I remember from our teenage arguments.

'I'm with her every day. Christ Almighty, why don't you bloody come back? Once in six months, that's all you can manage away from your important job at the precious solicitors.'

Her fingers are tapping against her thighs as if she's drumming out her words.

'You can get away on holiday though, can't you? She shows me the postcards. France, Italy, Spain. And the presents you send. Well done you.'

She turns towards me and purses her lips. There are lines etched across her forehead and I can see the grey at her temples.

She looks like our mother.

'You can't be watching her very carefully,' I say.

'What's that supposed to mean?'

'She's got a lighter. For her bloody smoker. And, as far as I can see, she hasn't burnt the place down yet, so how fucking bad can she be?'

My sister raises her arm. I step back. She turns back the cuff of her shirt and rolls her sleeve up. The bruises on her arm are purple birthmarks against her pale skin.

She turns back to the car and the slam of the door is loud in the afternoon air.

In the bee yard, I place my palms flat against the outer cover of the hive and feel the heat pulsing through the woodwork, strong as a beating heart. I wander from hive to hive. Some of the bees are agitated and the scouts are flying back and forth. I think they are getting ready to swarm. Mum is on her knees, trowel in hand, digging up weeds in the vegetable patch.

'This is a mess,' she says. 'Have you come to help?'

'Just for a while,' I say.

I kneel down next to her, disturbing small stones and hard,

dry worm castings. I can feel them through the material of my trousers. We work steadily. The chickweed and groundsel tug free easily and the loose soil crumbles inwards, filling the holes left by the roots.

'Don't forget to get all of the roots out,' she says, nodding towards the ragwort.

'I'll do it later. We need to go now,' I say.

I take a last look round the cottage and put away the lunch dishes we'd left on the draining board. I throw the rotting plums in the compost bin and swill out the washing up bowl. When I open the door to the sitting room, the scent from the lilies is overpowering, it fills my mouth, cloying at the back of my throat. I sit in her armchair, lean back and close my eyes. The shape of her is in the cushions. She is shouting, 'I'm not getting in. You wouldn't be doing this if my daughters were here. You wouldn't dare.'

I see myself uncurling her fingers, one by one, from their grip on the open door of the car, and feel the wool of her coat against the palm of my hand as I push down on her shoulders until, head bowed, she folds like a broken doll into the passenger seat.

After locking up, I wander down the garden. Out here, the air is still and heavy with the day's heat. I throw the lilies onto the heap of garden rubbish that has been dumped at the back of the vegetable patch for burning and, gathering up the pile of limp weeds we pulled out earlier, throw them on top of the flowers. Under the apple tree, I run my fingers through the feathery wild fennel growing in the grass. It leaves a warm, spicy trace of aniseed on my hands.

Around the plum tree, the air vibrates as if it is alive. The bees are swarming. Unnerved, I bat the stragglers away from my face. They sound anxious. There is panic in the frantic beat of their wings. Above me, they hang, cone-like, from a topmost branch, a rippling mass of gold and brown. The colours shift and shimmer against the green leaves, like the wind rushing through the heads of the ripening wheat.

Closed Season

EARLY JUNE. She walks with her dog on the Downs. The footpaths are all overgrown and tangled and, as she pushes through the undergrowth, tall spikes of purple foxgloves brush beads of moisture across her clothes. Everything has grown high and wild. Like the swollen seed heads of the grass on the bank opposite her cottage, the long stems of the foxgloves bend forward, hung with the mass of their flowers.

Over the last few weeks, resting on her bed during the day, she gazed through the window at the stalks of grass swaying in the strong winds. She thought about dragging her fingertips across them and imagined the spiky hairs catching against her skin. Now, tiny grass seeds stick to the dog, verdant specks on his black fur. She picks each one off. His coat is soft and warm, his dog-life beating strongly under her hands.

There is no one to see her. She walks, arms raised to avoid being stung by the towering nettles and, as she swings her hips, moving her body from side to side, the rucksack shifts against her back. Her polo shirt is old and out of shape, her jeans tucked into thick, ribbed socks. Poppies dot the edges of the rape fields, the colours sharp and concentrated. She knows where there is a lone, young stag. The animal has been spotted in the woods that cling to the hillside. Last week, in the shop, they were saying it had broken through some stock fencing and could be hurt. They told her the gamekeeper is after it. He might shoot it. He's only waiting for a closed season licence to come through.

On the phone to her daughter, after they had made plans for a birthday trip, she had spoken of finding the stag. Her daughter's reply was sharp. She must be mad to think of going up to the woods. It would be too much of a hike for her at the moment. *Honestly Mum, the path from the bridle road is almost covered by bracken and brambles. And good god, why can't you wait a bit? Mum?* She hadn't answered. The one thing she knows is that she wants to see the animal. Soon. And today, as she walks on the hills, the sun feels hot on her bare arms.

By the side of the track stands an old shepherd's hut. Its wheels are veiled by lace-headed cow parsley. Almost hidden amongst the grass, fragments of metal litter the ground. Rusty and sharp, it looks as if these pieces have been bitten from the hut's roof by voracious weather. It's at home here, this hut, rooted into the landscape. In its curving shadow, the air is cooler and, when she perches on a tree stump, the sudden chill chases across her arms. She sits on the clammy surface of the weathered wood, staring across the fields, hoping for an early glimpse of the stag. She is alive to any movement in the crops, any slight ripple in the wheat that would show her he was near.

The air settles around her. Birdsong, the hum of insects and the rustle of the dog in the brush, all seem distant as if the day is fading away from her. Yesterday evening, standing in her kitchen, her son had announced that, come January, she will be a grandma. In the telling, his voice had caught against the rush of words, reminding her of the boy he used to be. His arms around her, hugging her close, he had called her Grandma Maggie, whispering, 'You are pleased, aren't you, Mum?' in her ear.

'I'm too young,' she said. And laughed.

'Fifty-four's not young,' he said. His arms squeezed her tight. 'Oh, and the family grapevine says you're thinking of going up on the hills. You wouldn't do anything that silly, would you?'

And she had shaken her head against his chest, feeling a knot of tears sitting in her throat.

Later, after he had gone, she opened the cedar blanket box and unpacked the photograph albums. She sat on the floor with her legs crossed, her back resting against the end of her bed as she turned the pages of the last thirty-five years of her life. Years of holidays and barbecues, birthdays and Christmases, silly hats and first days at school. Pictures of her babies, now both grown up. And there, with the two children, were the two of them. She had looked through these glimpses of their life together until the evening light bled from the room.

She's interrupted by the dog pushing his muzzle under her hands. He has forced through the weeds, disturbing the viscous stench of a fox. The smell will cling around his head for the next few hours. It's time to move on and, as the dog disappears under a mantle of green, she follows the plume of his tail through the grasp of the undergrowth. Her daughter was right, this is hard going. More than once, her foot snags against hidden roots and, throwing her arms wide, she saves herself from falling, jarring her back in the process. From time to time, she feels a familiar jab of pain across her belly and stops to catch her breath. As she winds uphill, the dark nettles surrender to paler bracken, the young fronds unfurling across the track.

Then she is free, finding the dog waiting in a small clearing. Behind her, the footpath is hidden once more by the bracken and brambles, as if it's oblivious to her passing. Opening the rucksack, she takes out a bottle and pours a drink for the dog. While he laps, she frees two tablets from a foil strip and swallows them with a mouthful of the water. The liquid is warm and leaves a faint metallic taste in her mouth. She checks the time on her phone and sees there's a message.

Hi Grandma, here I am.

She's looking at a picture of her grandchild, such a scrap at the moment, a little question mark hidden amongst swirls of blacks and white.

As it leaves the clearing, the path falls sharply from the shoulder of the hill, follows the fence line beside a field of wheat and is lost as it turns into a copse. Before moving on, she scans the dappled ground beneath the trees, but sees only the young shoots of scrub growing up through the leaf mould. They set off, the dog staying close, brushing against her leg as they walk. His presence beside her is warm and solid. Her hand touches the top of his head. They reach the fence and, without warning, the dog tenses and springs forward. At the side of the path, the undergrowth parts and there is the stag.

Up from the edge of the field he rises and leaps into the wheat. He is glorious. She calls the dog to her side. The stag looks back over his shoulder, and for one heartbeat they all stand motionless. She dare not breathe. Sunlight catches the golden red of the animal's hide. Unable to stay still any longer, the dog slinks forward, a dark shadow on the ground, and the stag, propelled by ancient instinct, bounds away. She watches him flee, his body rising above the crops with each jump, the young wheat trembling behind him and the sun across the slope of his flank making him shine like a polished conker. Once more, tears unravel from the knot inside her and she wipes them on the hem of her shirt.

~

Some weeks later, she comes home from work to find the bank opposite her cottage has been mown. Cut grass lays in untidy clumps, scenting the air. A few forgotten stems fringe the post and rail fence. She shuts her front door on it all. While she was at work, her daughter-in-law has been in and taken the dog. His water bowl has been emptied and left, upside down, on the draining board. She sits at the kitchen table and stares at the corner where his bed should be. She thinks about the baby, wondering what it will feel like to hold the shape of a grandchild in her arms.

Upstairs, she puts on pyjamas and, with pillows stacked behind her, once more leafs through the photograph albums. Eventually, lights left on, she dozes. In the morning, without eating or drinking, she packs a bag and waits for her daughter to collect her.

~

After her operation, muddled images invade her drug-induced sleep. She sees the stag looking back at her, hears the crack of shotgun fire, and a jumble of voices calling out. When she opens her eyes, she finds her daughter holding her hand. They speak. She sleeps again. Waking in the night, she is alone, her mouth is dry, her throat sore and a heavy ache lies across her stomach. The darkness is punctured by pinpoints of light marking out the nurses' station, and the glare of a computer screen reflects in the window. A phone rings and, turning her head, she watches a nurse lift the receiver. When she wakes next, bands of morning sunlight cut across the walls and a young woman, slight and pretty, is standing beside the bed. A cup of tea is on the locker.

'Hello, Maggie. How do you feel?' the young nurse says.

She hates it in the hospital. She hates the whisper of rubber-soled shoes, the muted voices and the curtains screening her bed. She feels suffocated in the over-warm air. On her second morning, she is allowed to get up and sit in a chair. At first, the vinyl covering feels cool against her skin, but after a time she feels a slick of perspiration on the back of her thighs and stands, gripping the metal bed frame. She perches on the edge of the mattress unable to swing her feet onto the bed. This is how she remains, palms pressed onto her legs, until a care assistant arrives with the lunch. She resents her body for failing her.

The doctor has told her that, if she's lucky, her stay will be short, and she works hard on her recovery, walking up and down until the nurses tell her to rest. On her travels, the corridors are often busy and there is a never ending flow of people slipping around her. Once, stepping aside to let a group of students pass, she backs towards a large window and, turning, finds she can see the top of the Downs in the distance, a dark curve on the horizon. She visits the window every day. Although she can walk by herself, on the day she is discharged, her son takes her through the hospital in a wheelchair. She does not protest, after all she will not be driving for a while and he has come to take her home.

~

She spends her days reading, dealing with paperwork or pottering around the cottage. She has the French doors open, filling the room with warm summer air. Her meals are light. She makes omelettes, poaches salmon and eats the quiche her son has made. Gradually, she feels her strength returning. One night, woken by a clap of thunder, she stands at the window, curtains billowing around her, and watches forks of lightning slice through the sky above the hills. The dog, hearing her movement, steals into the room and sits at her feet. When she returns to bed, he jumps up alongside her and curls with his head lying across her legs. In the morning, she wipes raindrops from the sill.

The following Saturday, her children and their partners gather at the cottage to tidy her neglected garden. While they work, yanking nettles and pruning shrubs, she stakes her tomato plants, pinching out the side shoots and tying the stems with coarse jute twine. The sap leaves a pungent residue on her fingers, which she wipes away with a tissue. She no longer tires quickly, yet they insist she sits in the shade and hand her a newspaper which remains unopened on her lap.

'Don't you worry, Mum, just stay there with your feet up and watch,' her daughter says, passing round mid-morning coffee and hot bacon rolls. Her inability to drive, dig, lift or pull weeds is brought into question, and the relief in the gentle teasing is palpable, hanging in the air around them as they work. The dog runs back and forth offering his ball to anyone who stops for a moment. It is a day of laughter and lame jokes but, although she loves them, she finds herself glad when they leave late in the afternoon, squashed into their cars, amongst the bulging sacks of her garden rubbish.

The following day, she phones her neighbour and invites her to the cottage. They sit outside, shaded by a garden umbrella. She pours tea and talks about her grandchild. She has seen a new picture; her granddaughter had been revealed. A winter baby. They chat about children, friends in the village, the Harvest Festival and whether she will be up to making cakes for a charity stall. She is feeling better, she says. A bit cooped-up, she will be glad when her life is back to normal again. As they drink their tea, she wonders if there's any news of the stag.

'Such a shame, my dear,' her neighbour says. 'It had a piece of barbed wire caught around its leg. What a mess that made.' Her cup rattles as she places it back on the saucer. 'The wounds were infected. Nothing they could do but shoot it. The beginning of July it was, right when you went in.'

She takes the teapot from the tray and her hands are shaking. 'I'll pop some more water on this,' she says.

In the kitchen, she stands with her hands in the pockets of her trousers, leans back against the work top and waits for the kettle to boil. She closes her eyes and remembers how warm the day had been, the yellow rape, the splash of red poppies along the edges of the path and the stag leaping from the ground. On the floor, the dog is asleep in a patch of sunshine. She had walked for miles with him at her side.

When her neighbour leaves, she stacks the cups in the dishwasher and rinses the teapot. Back outside, she cuts sweet peas and fills glass jugs with the twisted stems of the purple and pink flowers taken from her garden. Unable to settle, she wanders through the cottage, tidying up books, a magazine, and shaking the cushions, until she finds herself in the hallway. Calling the dog, she grabs her keys from the hook.

She drives through the lanes to the car park. Here, at the foot of the Downs, the land is flat and the woods are cut through by gravelled paths to encourage families of Sunday walkers. She sits on a log seat watching the shadows lengthen. Birdsong. Midges swirl around her head. In places, patches of bracken have grown so tall she wishes she could stand beneath them, letting the fronds curl over her head. Voices and laughter. A couple wander by with a buggy. The dog, tongue out, flings himself panting at her feet. She should have brought a cardigan. It is not as warm in the shade of the trees as she expected. Returning home, she decides this outing is not something she will mention to anyone.

~

It's her birthday, and she travels to London with her daughter. They sit outside a Greek restaurant on Bankside, watching the Thames rush out towards the sea. Shingle beaches lay exposed as the water level falls lower. Above their heads, the Olympic rings hang on the arc of a bridge. People rush everywhere. Sunshine wraps around the city and the late summer heat rises up from the pavement. The day is saturated with the smells of the muddy river, traffic and lunchtime foods. They toast each other with glasses of cold white wine at eleven thirty in the morning. Her daughter takes a photograph and she is caught, forever, laughing at this decadence.

On the train home, as soon as they have swapped the buildings of the city for open fields, she closes her eyes and dozes. Noise recedes. Chatter, station announcements, the wheels against the track, all become indistinct. She is aware of movement, of the passengers in the aisle, and the momentum of the train. Half asleep, she thinks of the generations of men and women who have travelled the paths across the Downs and the families who have farmed the land. The hills hum with their tread and their footprints weave through the tracks, the ditches and the wooded plantings, like threads of homespun. She will go there tomorrow. The train slows for their station, her daughter touches her arm, and she wakes with a start.

❧

She is on the Downs again. In her absence everything has been cut back and tidied. The footpaths now run clean and true along the edges of the fields. The going is easy. From up here, she can gaze out across the coastal plain towards the sea. All around, giant rolls of baled straw rest in the stubble. Gulls have flown inland and settled on the ground. The dog runs, charging at the birds, and they rise up in a squabble of cries only to resettle the moment he has moved off. The air is crisp as an early autumn apple. She checks for buzzards soaring above the tree line. There's an arrogance in their calls, a strident assertion of life that rips across the sky. The hills draw her. She wants to stride out. She wants to feel the rise of the landscape beneath her feet.

The Last Taste of Summer

To tell the truth, Mum's call annoys me. It's the second time she's phoned me this evening. She's already told me she's going to my brother's for a fortnight. They'll need her to stay for a bit now the baby is here. Joe's paternity leave is over and the in-laws are leaving soon. Of course, she carries on to say, this visit is right when I usually make the jam for the harvest festival, so it's not ideal, but never mind. I agree with her. I'm not sure where this conversation is going, but whatever she thinks, I'm not making the jam. Perhaps, I say, there will be time for the jam before she leaves.

I'm trying to reassure her. Yes, I do know she makes jam every year, has done for as long as I can remember, but it won't hurt this once if she misses it. After all, she'll enjoy being with the baby. I'll catch up with Joe soon to see if they need me. I can always take some leave. There's a pause. I say, night, Mum. She says, well, that's good, dear, because I didn't want to bother you. Apparently, there'll be builders coming in to replace the flat roof. She did tell me, she says. It's been booked for ages, and they can't be put off. It has to be done this side of winter.

Right. This is all a bit short notice. Doesn't she realise it could be difficult to get the time off? I might have meetings or staff on leave. Jess, she says, I do know how busy you always are that's why I'm asking you tonight, then you have time to sort yourself out. You said you've got some leave. There's no need to be here the whole time I'm away, just the few days the men are here. What about asking next door to help, I suggest. At one time, when it was the Bakers, she would have, but now there are new people, and we don't really know them do we? Not to ask, anyway. Turns out, it's only going to be a few days.

Later that evening, I'm in pyjamas, sitting crossed legged on the sofa watching a film, picking the pepperoni from the remains of a pizza, when the phone rings again. My brother.

'I hear you're coming to the rescue. Thanks Jessie, appreciate it.'

I wipe my fingers on kitchen towel and put the plate to one side.

'We feel bad enough about the hoo-ha over the jam without stopping the roofers as well,' he says. 'Although you could crack on with the preserving. Joking aside, Little Sis, I owe you.' I can hear the laughter in his voice.

'Looks like Mum's got it all sorted out,' I say.

Cleaning my teeth before bed, I catch sight of myself in the mirror over the hand basin. Funny, even without any makeup, I look okay, perhaps a bit worried and fed up, but okay. I pull my mouth into a grimace and wrinkle my nose. Makes no difference, it doesn't make me smile. I feel like I've been boxed into a corner, and I hate myself for that.

It's not as if this will be the first time I've been back to the village. There are birthdays, bank holidays, Christmases and Easters to call me back, and of course we had Dad's funeral, but usually I try to limit my stays to a day or two here and there. And luckily, in the last few years, since Joe has moved, longer visits are spent at his house down on the coast. In any case, as I tell Mum, there's a lot more room at Joe's.

So here I am. Mid-September. Sussex. Four days max. I pack enough underwear, throw my waterproof jacket over my arm and shut the door on my flat.

It's bell ringing practice when I arrive. Every Monday. Six-thirty start. Nothing changes. I turn into the lane and drive past the church towards the cottage. Cars line the verge and I'm forced into second gear to manoeuvre past. There are even a couple of vehicles parked on the gravel turn-around by the lychgate. Mum says it's becoming a bit of a problem, but thinking back to when Joe and I were young, to the weddings, burials and all the other comings and goings at St Mary's, it seems like it has always been this way.

The front door opens after a bit of a shove and I grab the post from the mat. I still have my own key; the same one Dad gave me when I was twelve. Jess, he said, handing it over, you're almost a grown-up now. In the hall, an assortment of coats hang on brass hooks over the radiator, hats on the shelf above, shoes and boots on the rack below. I drop my weekend bag by the stairs, kick off my trainers and walk through to the kitchen. The late sun soaks the room, warming the tiled floor under my feet. The local paper is folded on the worktop and a dozen jars are ranked upside down on the draining board, their lids in a pile by the side. I slide them out of the way, lean across and open the window over the sink. There is a rush of evening air from the garden and the room fills with birdsong, the *tik tik* of a robin and the monotonous cooing of collared doves. Above it all, there's the peel of the church bells.

In the centre of the table, no doubt left so I can't miss them, are three bags of golden granulated sugar, a bottle of lemon juice and Mum's old recipe book, its torn dustcover mended with now yellowing Sellotape. Next to them, the corner trapped under a terracotta pot of early, red cyclamen, lays a note, the loops and curls of Mum's handwriting telling me that the roofers will be here at eight in the morning unless it rains. She has made me a shepherd's pie and left it in the fridge. My favourite. And to please let her know when I have arrived. I'm grinning when I put the dish in the oven.

The phone rings whilst I'm in the garage searching for peas in the freezer. Slamming the lid down, I run inside to answer.

'Hello dear, it's Mrs Holmes. I saw you drive round the corner earlier and I thought, I must give Jessica a call to see how she is.'

'I'm fine, Mrs Holmes. How are – '

'We don't see enough of you, but your mum keeps us all in the loop with your goings on. She's so proud of you, up there in the city and doing so well. Doesn't seem longer than yesterday when you went. Who'd have thought it, you a manager, in charge of an office. Advertising isn't it, dear? And then, before you know it, she's a grandma and you an auntie.'

'Yes, it's great. We're all very pleased. They're – '

'And you're only at home for a few days? The builders, isn't it? Must be boring for you down here on your own. I said to your mum, shame there's no young man on the scene for her to bring down, because there's no one much left in the village to catch up with now all the youngsters have grown up and gone.'

I walk into the kitchen and sit on the edge of a chair with my elbows on the table.

'Well, that's house prices, way too expensive here nowadays. You remember my grandson Peter, don't you – ever so keen on him, you were. He was at school with your Joe? He's moved now. I expect you know that. Your mum will have kept you up to date. He's still local, mind.'

'Right. I think I can hear my mobile, Mrs Holmes. I'd better – '

'Showed me that lovely photo of you on your holidays, she did. Italy wasn't it? I'd know you anywhere. She hasn't changed a bit, I said. Jessica looks just the same as when she was at school, what with that red hair and all those freckles. Still, I often think back to that last summer. So wild you all were.'

The fridge hums. A fly is batting against the window pane.

'Drove us mad with your ways. And the rows. I'd say to your mum, don't you worry, when you get to my age you've seen it all before. She'll grow out of it. They all do. I was right, wasn't I, dear?'

After I've eaten, and shadows are creeping across the wooden floor, I sit in the living room, the television on low and a glass of wine in my hand. Old Mrs Holmes is right. It had been a difficult summer. Yes, that's how I remember it. Difficult. I was desperate to leave, to get out and go up to London. Mum and Dad were frantic with worry, trying to understand, trying to stop me. I knew people who had gone up there, I told them. Friends of mine, people they didn't know. I had savings. For god's sake, I was sixteen, I would get a job.

Bloody stupid, boring village, full of nosey, boring people. I hate it here, I'd shouted. There was nowhere to go and nothing to do. That was all I said, no other explanation. I turned away and refused to speak to them, trailing my unhappiness around the cottage like a bad smell. In the end, they helped. I packed my stuff and let them drive me to West London, to the room in the shared house that I'd found. The room that they'd paid the deposit on. It was my battle to get free and I thought I'd won.

I drink some wine. The news begins on the television, I turn it off. Perhaps it's a bit late to give Joe a call but I do it anyway, calling his mobile to say I've arrived, make sure the baby is doing well and tell him to thank Mum for the shepherd's pie. She's gone to bed, so I don't get a chance to speak to her. Joe's laughing when he asks if I've made the jam yet, and reminds me of the year I was stung by a wasp while picking the fruit. Yes, I say, I remember, my cheek swelled up and it bloody hurt. But who was it that burnt his mouth eating hot jam from the spoon? Then I tell him about Mrs Holmes. He's glad to hear the grapevine is still thriving. We both say goodnight. I don't mention Peter.

That summer, that difficult summer. It was Joe, back from his travels, who'd come up to see me. Joe, who told me how frightened our parents had been. He called me selfish, a spoilt little brat. He stood in my room, suntanned and skinny, his backpack on the floor by his feet, refusing to sit down, and let me know terrified they'd been. Our parents, thinking they might lose me forever. What the hell had happened? How could I have treated them like shit? I shouted back. Asked what the fuck he knew, after all, he hadn't been there, he'd been off seeing the world. He was disappointed in me – was not expecting me to be jealous. Surely it had been about more than that, he wanted to know. I called him a pompous prick. I remember how flat and hollow I sounded. We argued, as only siblings can, with spiteful accuracy. Afterwards, when things were calmer, we went out for food. Pompous prick. And, sitting on plastic seats under fluorescent strip lighting in an indistinguishable cafe with our burgers in throwaway containers, we both began to laugh at that.

The room is dark now. I have no idea how long I've been here, my wine finished and the phone in my lap. Maybe it won't be so bad, these few days back home. All I need to do is keep busy and, with luck, I can be gone by sometime Thursday. As I reach to turn on a lamp, there's a crash in the kitchen. One of the jars has toppled from the draining board and smashed into the sink. I shut the window and close the blind before gathering up the shards of glass and parcelling them into sheets of newspaper.

I wake early. In the corner of the room, the bookcase still holds some of my battered paperbacks, a couple of Disney ornaments and an old desk lamp. Little else remains of my childhood belongings. I'm glad Mum has had the room redecorated. I lie on my back and watch the patterns of morning light spread across the walls of my bedroom.

Before I've eaten breakfast, the roofers arrive and rolls of felt, sheets of deck-boarding, ladders and a tar pot have been unloaded. Mum phones. Just to check, dear. Although she knows I'll be fine. Have I decided what to do all day because it sounds very noisy? She can't hear the half of it. Overhead, hollow footsteps compete with the thumps of a hammer and the crack of splintering wood. She's right, there's no way I'm staying here. I find a plastic tub in the cupboard, snatch an old gardening coat from the peg in the hall, take coffee outside for the roofers and tell them I'll be gone for a while.

In the churchyard, I stop beside Dad's memorial plaque. The stone is clean, the grass around it clipped, and I smile at another pot of cyclamen adding a splash of colour. I don't stay long, I never do, and climbing the stile in the far corner of the cemetery, I stare out beyond the boundary of old yew across acres of arable farmland, its borders framed with scruffy thickets of elder and hawthorn. The same well-worn track leads me down to the set-aside edges, where the brambles grow thick and high and summer-ripe berries sit proud above the thorns.

To avoid the whip of the bramble canes, I move with care, my fingers purpling as I pick the fat fruit. How many years has it been since I've done this? At my feet, the tub is half full, and I realise it could take hours to gather enough for Mum's jam. Why didn't I think to bring a flask? By late morning, I've dumped Mum's jacket at the side of the path. The sun-warmed air is still, the heat trapped between the hedgerows is thick with the drone of wasps, and the brambles are flecked yellow with resting anglewings. Working my way along the bushes, I lean in as far as I dare, trying not to scratch my arms.

I hear laughter before I see anyone. A couple are striding along towards me, their footsteps echoing on the hard, clay ground. The woman is wearing a waxed gilet, her black leggings tucked into boots, and the man, tall, is in a marl grey t-shirt and faded jeans. There's something about him. No. Surely not. I step back into the shelter of the hedgerow, putting out my hand as if to stop myself falling. This can't be happening. But it is, and my god, I would have known him anywhere. Peter

Summer. Me, sixteen. Him, eighteen. The abandoned footpath over the railway bridge and the two of us lying together in the long, cool grass, our limbs smooth and tanned. I remember how heavy and languorous my body felt while I lay still, waiting for the touch of his fingertips. The hours had been torpid with the day's heat, and the sky, bright blue, streaked with spent vapour trails. We drank cider, followed by rough, cheap vodka and, right at this moment, I can almost smell the sweet curl of smoke from our joint.

'Morning. Lovely day. Aren't we lucky?' he says, nodding as they draw level.

He sounds the same. No, that's ridiculous, yet his voice seems as familiar to me as if I had heard it yesterday.

'Morning,' I say.

Thank god. He hasn't seen me, not really seen me. Not seen me enough to recognise me. No reason to stop and chat. I watch as he goes past, my body protected by the bushes, my hands shaking. He looks back, a smile on his face. Please, no. And retraces his steps.

'Jessie? It is you, isn't it? You remember me? Peter. Peter Holmes. How long has it been?'

‘Hi. Yes, of course. It’s been years,’ I say.

‘Good to see you. How are you?’

‘Okay. Great. I’m doing great.’ Surely now he’ll move on.

‘Let me think. Didn’t Gran mention you’d gone to London? She usually keeps me posted with all the news. Still there, aren’t you?’ He turns to the woman at his side. ‘Darling, I’ve mentioned the summer before I went to college, told you how it all got a bit wild. Well, this is Jess, Joe’s sister.’

For a moment, his grin makes me sixteen again.

‘Despite what I’ve told her about my misspent youth, she still married poor old Peter.’ And looking from his wife to me, he laughs. I don’t join in.

He places his hand on my arm. I try to step back.

‘Too many girls, way too much drinking and a shed load of smoking.’

Christ. He’s inviting me to share these jokes. He expects me to. My skin crawls. Through my t-shirt, the brambles press against my back.

‘I’m sure Jess doesn’t remember all that nonsense,’ his wife says, taking his hand from my arm. With a short laugh, she links her fingers through his.

‘Not proud of it. But Joe, he went off to see the world, and then Jessie, she upped and ran off to the city. You two were the free spirits, Jessie. You know, I envied you both so much for getting out.’ He glances at his watch. ‘We must go. Running a tad late, and you know my Gran, lunch will be waiting. Look, it would be great if we could meet up while you’re back. Catch up. Have a drink?’

For a moment, I don’t answer. How many hours had I spent as a teenager waiting to hear him say something like this? And when, at last, he had, how quickly I agreed to meet him, choosing my clothes with care and stealing unnoticed from the cottage.

‘I don’t think so. I’m only here for a couple more days,’ I say.

‘Shame. No problem. It was good seeing you. Say hi to Joe.’

As they walk away, a snatch of their conversation drifts back.

‘Off my head. No bloody idea what was going on most of the time back then.’

When I'm sure they're gone, and all I can hear is the craw of wheeling crows and the drone of wasps feeding amongst the blackberries, I put the lid on the tub, grab Mum's jacket and make my way back to the cottage.

Peter. I doubt if he remembers the arch of red bricks, rusted with orange lichen, the rumble of the train on the tracks below us, or the damp, foul stink of a nearby animal den. Yet, when I think back, I can still feel the fumble of his hands and the way his body shifted across me, forcing me down into the undergrowth. I remember waking, the ground hard under my hip, my head thick, thoughts blurred, and seeing a pile of empty bottles thrown amongst the stinging nettles. And try as I might, I can't forget that at sixteen years old all I had been left with was the raw taste of the cheap alcohol in the back of my throat and the musty smell of his sweat on my skin.

In the early hours before sunrise, I make coffee. I'd slept in fits and starts, my dreams full of raised voices. All of them, Mum, Joe, Mrs Holmes, Peter, filling my mind full of conversations that never happened and accusations that were never voiced. As the light streaks across the sky, I sit at the kitchen table and, without reading, turn the pages of Mum's recipe book.

By eight, I'm showered, dressed and leaning against the frame in the back doorway. I eat toast watching a pair of chaffinches poke around for insects under the hedge. I brush off my plate and the birds bob forward pecking up the crumbs. Yesterday, I abandoned the tub of blackberries, dumping it on the worktop, but now, this morning, I've decided to make the jam. I place a colander on the draining board, fill the sink with cold water, and lift the lid, releasing a smell of rot. The berries are covered in a rat-grey fungus. At the bottom of the tub, the fruit are sitting in a pool of juice as thick and dark as an expensive merlot, but no doubt with the taste of cheap vinegar. Tears thicken in the back of my throat.

There's a knock.

'Any chance of a coffee, love?' One of the builders, mugs in hand, is standing in the doorway.

He's smiling, walking towards me, and as he glances in the tub he says, 'Put the lid on and left 'em? Shame. No air. Makes them ferment.'

While the kettle boils, he sorts through the fruit, putting the rotten berries on the draining board and tipping the rest into the colander.

'Look, they're not all spoilt. Some of them are okay,' he says.

It takes me about an hour and, as the fruit heats in the pan, I rummage through the drawers looking for labels. As I look, Mum's kitchen fills with the warmth of hot sugar and the sharp smell of the blackberries.

When the jam is cooked, dropping, hot and viscous, like molten glass from the spoon, I skim the top and, like Mum has always done, swirl a knob of deep yellow butter through the boiling mass to settle the last of the scum. I pour the thick, cooling liquid into four jars and seal each one with a disc of waxed paper under the lid. The phone rings as I am about to stick on the labels. Mum. To see what I'm doing. Not much, I tell her. When she's gone, I label the jars. I'm done. I line the pots up on the kitchen table and, gem-like, they catch the last of the morning sun.

Bit by bit, I begin to clear up, filling the preserving pan with hot, soapy water and standing it in the sink. The leftover sugar goes into a canister and the worktop is wiped down. I lift up the colander ready to wash it, and there, laying on its own at the bottom, is a blackberry. One missed fruit. The berry is sweet, and when I bite it the juice is clean and fresh, like the last taste of summer.

Across to Halnaker

Tilting at Windmills

I'M MORE AT peace now. I no longer make drinks in the middle of the night or sit in the dark listening to the traffic, losing hours as the tea goes cold.

The night before I leave, I lay my clothes out across the top of the blanket box: underwear, jeans, a red polo neck and a pair of hiking socks, still partnered at the top by a cardboard tag. The ribbing feels thick and reassuring in my hand and, foolishly, I feel they have lingered in the drawer, waiting for this moment. Tomorrow will be another day of November damp, so I add a padded coat to the pile. I packed my rucksack last Sunday, popped the diary on top, and stood the bag in the corner of the sitting room. Since then the days have rushed past.

With my hand on the light switch, old doubts creep back and I'm unable to shut the door and go to bed. I don't speak to other people about it. Some things, like diaries, should be kept private. I hear my own breathing, rasping in the quiet room. The familiar racing of my heart begins, and I press two fingers against my wrist checking the beat of my pulse.

I'll sleep downstairs. There's a fleece blanket on the back of the sofa for times like this, besides it comforts me to see the rucksack waiting for the morning. With the curtains open, the streetlight pools onto the rug and passing cars cast beams across the walls.

When I wake, the room is submerged in moonlight. All the furniture seems larger and displaced, as if each piece has drifted on a gentle current. There are stars in the sky. Looking out of the window, I murmur the names of constellations. The Great Bear. Taurus. Orion. After all these years, and no matter how many times you've told me, I still can't recognise them. Not on my own. My breath clouds the glass and I find I've etched my name, *Evie*, on the pane.

Minutes slip past as I stand in the shower letting the hot water wash aches from my shoulders. There's no point in leaving too early. It's only a couple of hours drive, and when I get there, I'm hoping for an easy walk. Thank goodness, you made a note of the way.

Back at the window, I stare between the rooftops, watching the winking lights of a plane travel high and away. Words twist together through my thoughts, fragments of a poem you wrote in your diary. I know each line by heart.

I leave the clutter of the city, driving until I see the rising bulk of the South Downs closing in. Everywhere is empty. I'm wrong-footed in the countryside.

When I reach Halnaker, I spot the house. The house, remember? There it is sitting right on the main road opposite a lay-by. Estate agent jargon sneaks into my head: *A charming detached property in a rural setting.* Although the front door has been painted a different colour, I would recognise that house anywhere. Red-bricked and square, it sits with the mass of the chalk hillside glowering over lawns too large for a Flymo. I'd come across the details hidden at the back of your desk, clipped to a note from your mum. Recalled accusations worry at me. I'd wondered why she sent them. Didn't she understand, with the hours I worked we needed to live in the city. What a troubled day of raised voices it had been. Whatever she thought, we'd made no plans to move.

The signpost says it's a hike of three quarters of a mile to the windmill. I'm in the right place. And when I stand, with the car behind me in the lay-by, I think about how many times you've been here, in the very same spot. Strange how I never thought about that before. You've noted everything down, so I know the track runs forward under a canopy of overhanging trees and follows the route of the old Roman Road, yet I can't see any of this from where I'm parked. Do you remember how disappointed I was when you gave me the walking boots for my twenty-third? Well, can you believe I'm using them at last, after all this time?

The going is easy at first. A broad path leads up between two cottages, the hedges surrendering to grass-covered banks. I'm encouraged by the occasional hum of traffic. Don't worry you'd tell me, no doubt with a grin, civilisation is still nearby. Ahead, the tunnel of trees is barred by a metal gate. I might not get any further.

I missed it at first, but there's a stile to my right, covered in part by an elder sapling. A few berries remain, hanging in shabby black clusters amongst the dying leaves. Elders to keep the devil away, or so your mother says. She always has a lot to say, your mother.

The stile is greasy, and I clutch the upright post, feeling the backpack shift against me. Further on, the track climbs the bank, running uphill, parallel to the old road. It's spiteful underfoot. Fallen leaves hide slippery tree roots and sharp, exposed flint. I pass a field of donkeys. They interrupt their grazing to glance at me with old eyes, but I'm soon dismissed in favour of cropping at the grass.

The landscape takes me on. Sheer-faced, the sides of a disused chalk pit drop away from the edge of the path. Water has collected at the bottom of the bowl and, from here, the pool appears black and deep. There's only a barbed wire fence covered with snarls of brambles to stop me plunging over the edge.

Another stile and then I'm standing on a path between more fields. You said there's a glimpse of the windmill from here, but I'm not tall enough to see past the boundary hedge. I climb back up and, holding tight, turn to face the hill.

I can see why you love her. Her white cap and two sails are bold against the blue of the sky, and her body is shielded by the rise of the land, as if she's peeping over the slope of the Downs. I carry on up to meet her at last.

When I reach the top, irrational questions bombard me. Was she expecting me? Did she guess that I would come to find her? I look back across empty farmland. I'm wrong-footed again. Me, I need the hustle of people, the buzz in the air when you surface from the underground. I like the push and shove of it all. In the rise and fall of this open space, there is only me and her. And this is her territory.

Up close, she is old, a faded beauty, patched with yellow lichen. Her shabby brickwork is exposed by missing hang tiles and her mortar is crumbling. Above her empty doorway, a plaque reads:

This ancient landmark was restored in the year 1934 by Sir William Bird of Eartham in memory of his wife. I lean the rucksack against the doorjamb and step inside. The rush of the wind is silenced by her thick, brick walls. Small pebbles shift under the impact of my boots and the crunch of gravel as I land is swallowed by four storeys of vacant space above my head.

Other people have been here.

There are empty firework boxes inside her tower. They're not littered around, forgotten in the aftermath of some wild party. No, they're stacked in a pile, the up-turned lids angled close against the wall and, balanced on top, a heap of rocket launching tubes. Roman Candle. Golden Fountain. Scarlet Fury. All their promises of brilliant explosions spent.

I knock my toe against the bottom box, releasing the dank smell of puddle water. The cardboard is wet, offering no resistance as it bows inwards over the curve of my boot. Layers of compacted paper split with a sigh, leaving flecks of grey clinging to the new, brown leather. This is no place for a party. I kick harder. The whole lot lifts from the floor and, for a second or two, holds its shape like an illusionist's trick. The boxes fall back, the impact splitting them apart. I kick again, flinging pieces of cardboard against the wall. And again. I don't stop until the gravel is covered in fragments of cardboard, and so many scattered words.

I picture the partygoers all around the windmill, their voices echoing inside her ancient belly. They dance across the grassland, their imprints sloughed at the same time as their discarded rubbish. Back outside, I sit on the bench and open the diary.

Saturday June 1st. A beautiful day. Blue sky. Scudding clouds. A peregrine dipping and gliding over Denge Bottom and Red Copse. Lost sight of him when he plunged down into Halnaker Park. Damp earth. They've cut the scrub back.

She's behind me, the bulk of her empty tower casting a shadow across the crest of the hill. Fields roll away below us. In the valleys, trees still blaze with their autumn reds and yellows, patched in places by squares of evergreen pines, like the flag of some unknown country spread across the landscape. From my seat, I hear your voice, strong and clear above the buffeting wind, introducing me to your friends. Red Copse. Halnaker Park. Denge Bottom.

Perhaps I should have phoned your mum; told her I was coming here. Yet whenever we meet, she's cold towards me, wearing her disapproval like a rash. I'm not countrified. You think I'm exaggerating, that I imagine the slights and the barbed comments, that I'm fighting a war that isn't there, fighting with an imaginary foe. But I bet she still tells her friends how disappointing it is to have a daughter-in-law like me. A high-flyer. Tells them how I caught her son at university and kept him away. She's never understood me. Never understood us. You know how I thrive on the energy of the city. How it excites me. And you, well you could teach English anywhere.

That's what you said.

I stand and take the wooden box from the rucksack. My hands shake and I struggle to loosen the lid. Before I can change my mind, I throw the contents high into the air. I whisper the poem, your poem, stumbling on the second verse, and my words are carried up and over the hillside. For a moment, the light grey ash drifts towards the earth, then the wind, tugging at the heads of the dying grasses, snatches you up and bears you away.

The windmill is blurred through my tears, and I like her softer image. I turn to go, but I can't leave her like this. Again, I jump down into the tower and start to gather all the scraps of cardboard, cramming them into my bag. When I'm done, I balance the empty wooden box on top, along with your diary. I place my hand on the warm bricks, the old mortar rough beneath my fingers.

Outside, across the coastal plain, the horizon glistens and there's the sea, no more than a band of shifting silver in the distance. The air is cool and damp. It carries the scent of wood smoke. Going down is easier. I walk quickly and my footsteps are lighter.

I stop on the path above the chalk quarry. Far below, the scars of derelict workings are healing under a growth of brushwood and trees. Closer, from in the hawthorn scrub, a blackbird sings and I try to spot him amongst the branches. And there, tight amongst the thorns, bright red haws speckle the hedgerow.

The Broom Maker

He leaves his kitchen at first light, closing the door on the breakfast dishes left in the sink. The morning sky is streaked with cloud and he pauses to watch the globe of the winter sun rise above the horizon. Under his arm, held tight against his chest, he carries a flask of coffee and, in his hand, a packet of sandwiches wrapped in tin foil. Outside, the air is cold. The night's frost has veiled the hedgerow, softening the stark outline of the hawthorn. In the rime on the grass, the tracks of a fox cross the corner of the field. Sitting in his pickup, he slips a tobacco pouch from his pocket and rolls a cigarette, pulling and tucking the tobacco with the tips of his fingers. When he drives off down the lane, the tang of Golden Virginia fills the cab.

As usual, he stops at the village store. He gets in early, in the quiet hour before the rush of school mums, when there is time to gather up gossip along with his bread, tobacco and milk. As a boy, he spent his pocket money on sweets from jars stacked behind the counter, walking home up the hill with the bulk of a gobstopper tucked in his cheek and a bag of cola cubes, flying saucers or liquorice laces clutched in his hand. Today, the shop is busy. A delivery of frozen food stands as if forgotten by the freezers. They are short-staffed and no one has a moment to chat. Before he pays, he plucks a copy of the *Chichester Observer* from a pile on the floor.

He turns off the road at the National Trust signpost, jumps out and unlocks the padlock, shoving the heavy gate aside and looping the chain around the post to hold it open. Back in the truck, he drives slowly through the parkland. Woods of birch, elm and hazel spread out either side of the lane, and the rise of a medieval pale curves away in front of him, like the ridge of a backbone. Fenceless, the pale no longer forms a barrier and, over the centuries, passing deer have cut paths across the top of the mound. In the spring, under a canopy of bright new leaves, these woods will be covered in bluebells. Thousands of spikes will push up through the leaf mould and, when they are disturbed, fill the air with a tart, green scent. But now, at the end of January, a ground mist creeps round the bases of the trees, blankets the undergrowth and dampens the russet fronds of the dead bracken at the foot of the pale. He steers with care, the old flint and brick track is rutted and, overnight, the puddles have frozen, hiding the potholes under a covering of ice.

When he reaches the coppice, he parks beside a stand of holly and, before leaving the truck to start work, smokes another roll-up and drinks coffee from his flask. A fieldfare hops from branch to branch, the black tip of its tail flicking and its yellow beak jabbing as it feasts on the fat, red berries. The local paper is folded on the seat beside him and he glances at the headlines, 'Chichester traders report bumper Christmas sales'. It had been a good year for him. He enjoyed setting up his stand at farmers' markets and craft fairs across the county. There was camaraderie amongst the stallholders. When it rained, they were wet. When the wind blew sharp, they were cold. When a crowd bustled around with their money in their hands, they were happy.

This last year, he had diversified, so hobby horses, their heads covered in brightly painted spots, polished wooden stools and Sussex trugs stood on the stall alongside his handmade besom brooms. To entice the customers, there were door wreaths and decorations made from discarded twigs and embellished with pine cones and cinnamon sticks. He tied the decorations with tartan ribbons and hung them from a plywood stand. The stall looked great. He had not anticipated that his work would be so popular, nor realised that he would sell so many brooms. By the beginning of December, he was working into the night to complete all the Christmas orders he had taken for the besoms.

His breath hangs in the cold morning air. When he leans in to collect his tools from the bed of his truck, a chill crawls across the back of his neck. In the coppice, he bends low over a birch stump, slicing through the stems with his billhook and throwing them to the side. The weather through the year has been kind, the growth of the wood strong, and he is swift and economical in his cutting, moving with practised ease from stump to stump.

At lunchtime, he stops, gathers the cut twigs and loads them into the back of the truck. He eats his sandwiches and, resting the local paper against the steering wheel, reads about the closure of village pubs, funding for the library service, the success of the rugby teams, and the death of a woman he knew. He throws the dregs of his coffee through the open window, rolls a cigarette and reads the announcement again.

After her marriage to Simon Robbins, Erica Williams Robbins left the area in 1993. However, her ashes will be returned to the village she loved. There will be a short memorial service in St Mary's Church on Friday 25th January at eleven thirty, followed by a celebration of her life in the village hall. Her family invite all who knew her to attend.

The sky is clear, sliced only by the white line of a vapour trail. As he watches the plane, he remembers a school trip to Venice when he was sixteen, the shabby beauty of the buildings, their crumbling facades, the rounded arches of the bridges and the smell of the dark canals that threaded through the city. And there was James. *I want to discover what real Venetians love, Mikey,* James had said to him, throwing an arm across his shoulder. Then the pair of them turned away and left the rest of their classmates to wander St Mark's Square and the Rialto Bridge without them.

It was James, in acid wash jeans and a tight white t-shirt, who led him through narrow backstreets strung with washing lines and into hidden piazzas. It was James who said they should have beers, and made the waiter laugh with tourist Italian. James who grabbed Mike's wrist, skin against skin, to point out the icon standing in a niche, the vivid blue dress of the Virgin Mary a brilliant dash against the fresh cream plasterwork.

The plane is long gone, leaving the vapour trail feathering the sky. Cigarette finished, he rubs his fingers across his eyes and glances over to the ancient rise of the pale, where bedraggled stems of willowherb and hogweed have remained through the winter, held in place by the snarl of brambles. He folds the paper, steps from his truck and returns to his work in the coppice.

His sister hangs her coat on the hook by the back door.

'Get the kettle on,' she says, placing her keys and bag on the table. 'How's it going?'

'All good. Rugby's going well. Under fourteens could win the cup this season. Robbie's doing great.'

He reaches down two mugs and adds a teabag to each.

'Really, Gracie, he's a good, solid player. And how's my niece doing?'

'Fine, wants her room decorated. Purple. I said pink.' She pulls a paint chart from her bag.

'Let her have what she wants. I'll paint it.'

She points at a square on the chart. 'She's having pink.'

'Lunch on Sunday? My turn. I'll do beef.'

'And apple crumble?'

As he pours water on their tea, she asks, 'Have you heard about Erica Williams?'

He can hear the ticking of the kitchen clock from its place on the wall behind him and when, without looking at her, he puts the mugs down on the table, the knock of china against wood seems loud.

'I'll need to make more besoms this year. Start full-time in April, as soon as the coppicing is finished.'

'What do you reckon? Bit of a surprise, burying her ashes here after twenty years.'

'I saw the notice in the paper,' he says, stirring sugar into his tea.

'Right. It's on Friday. James will come back for it, no doubt. Got any bikkies?'

He reaches for the biscuits and slides the tin across the table. On the lid, the words 'Family Assortment' are spelled out in a big, white smile.

'Mike?'

'I expect.'

'Oh god, look at the time,' she says, grabbing her keys and bag. 'Need to get the kids.'

He takes her coat down and holds it while she slips her arms in. She kisses his cheek. 'The funeral. You'll go?'

He shrugs.

When she has left, he goes upstairs to change. With his work clothes dumped on the bathroom floor, he stands, wearing only his boxer shorts, in front of the hand basin. He is greying at the temples and, for some time now, has let the girl at the salon run the clippers over his hair to keep it tidy. Has he changed? Of course he has. How much? He is still slender with legs long and a stomach as flat as when he and James were teenagers. He runs his fingers across his chest, tracing the ridge of hard muscles.

Rolling a can of shaving foam between his palms, he thinks his hands are large and ungainly. They might be strong and capable when he is working, but there is no doubt they are rough, outdoor hands. Drawing the razor across the stubble on his face, he nicks the skin and a drop of blood runs slowly down his cheek. He blots it with a scrap of tissue.

Dressed, he sits on the edge of the bed and takes a letter from the drawer in his bedside table. How impatient he had been for this to arrive. Turning the envelope in his hands, he smiles at the scrawl of his name in deep green ink. November 1991. He hasn't looked at it in years, hasn't slipped the pages free and gazed at the once familiar writing.

I did it, Mikey. I'm here, in London, at last. You'll come up and visit won't you, like we planned?

He is almost late for midweek rugby practice, only just finishing setting out the training cones as the children arrive. He hands out tabards and checks laces are tied. The children call him Coach and, for an hour and a half, he runs up and down shouting advice and encouragement. At the end of the session, when the team places are finalised, he passes round sheets of instructions for the matches at the weekend.

The children group together under the floodlights, waiting for their parents. Their chatter, as high pitched and busy as starlings, carries on the cold evening air as he helps his neighbour gather kit bags into the boot of her car.

'Thanks, Mike,' she says. 'Have you heard about Erica Williams?'

'I've heard. There, that's the last of them.' He shuts the boot.

'You were always great friends. You and James. At school. Weren't you?'

'I suppose. Long time ago. Right, see you at the match.'

'God, he was a handsome boy. All of us girls were after him. Remember?'

'I remember.'

'And clever. University.'

'Yeah.'

'They say in the shop, he'll be here for the service and he's staying overnight at The Swan.' She packs the children into the car, checking seat belts and handing out snacks.

'Right.'

'It'll be good to catch up, even under these circumstances. See how he's doing. He married, didn't he?'

'Not sure. I need to get a move on. Night.'

'Couple of kids, I think. Mind you, can't say I wasn't surprised. There was that talk going around. But by then the family had moved. You'll be going, won't you? You really were such good friends, the two of you. Inseparable.'

It's mad here. Last week we went to the Natural History Museum. There's an exhibition of wildlife photography. You'd love it.

'Maybe. I've got work. You know how it is.'

'Yeah, it's a bit short notice.'

Around him voices shout 'good night', doors slam and the car park empties.

When you come up, I'll get us tickets for Twickenham and we'll go on the bus.

The moon is full and the light floods the fields as if it were day. The scent of his tobacco surrounds him as he folds his arms and leans them on the top rail of the fence, a cigarette between his fingers. The wind is stronger now. It moves among the branches of the trees. Behind him, the leaves of the holly scratch against the brickwork of the shed. He can taste the cold in the air. The frost will be heavy tonight. Where the fences meet at the corner of the field, he spots a flash of movement. A fox, the fur on its throat and chest a blaze of white in the undergrowth. He grinds the end of his roll-up under his heel.

He works quietly, seated on his broom horse, the cold stinging his cheeks and the light from the overhead bulbs spilling out of the open doorway into the night. With the curved blade of his draw knife, he strips the bark from a length of hazel and begins to shape the broom handle. Shavings fall around his feet, curling like question marks on the ground. The air is filled with the resinous scent of fresh bare wood. When the handle is smooth, he cuts one end to a point with an axe. Over the years, the blows from his axe have marked the cutting stump he uses until the surface has become lined and weathered like the skin on his hands.

From a pile of brushwood, he gathers an armful of twigs for the broom head. As he rolls them on his knees, he wonders what James was doing two years ago on the day he cut this birch from the coppice. He wonders if James, moving through his life in London, ever stops, perhaps in a restaurant or a theatre foyer, to think about him. Does James picture him at work, collecting the wood? Does he remember how it had been, the two of them talking, rolling cigarettes, making plans? Does he remember lying on the cool bracken in their secret place beneath the trees, their skin perfumed by the damp earth, the dappled light patterning their bare chests? When he is satisfied with the shape and heft of the besom, he secures the head, winding strands of galvanised wire tightly around the bundle of twigs and twisting the sharp ends safely together.

Four o'clock. It is not worth going to bed. The envelope sits on the kitchen table. He draws the letter free, and smooths the creases.

November 1991. Dear Mikey, I did it. I'm here. Freedom at last. I'm glad I didn't get into Halls now, I like being out on a limb. It's a bit weird being the only bloke living with four girls. They've got their stuff everywhere. But it's working out. I've told them all about you. When you come up, you can sleep in my room. It'll be okay, no one gives a damn here. Everything is cool. Can't wait to show you around.

He makes coffee, opens the back door and steps out into the cold. It's a strange time, he thinks, this margin of winter darkness between night and day. The moon had been bright, but while he was inside, a bank of cloud has built, dimming the sharp outlines of the hedges and fences. In his workshop, he takes a dustpan and brush and sweeps the shavings from the floor. With a whetstone held in the clamp of the broom horse, he sharpens the curved blade of his knife, drawing it against the ridges of the stone until the edge is honed and true. He collects a new pile of seasoned birch twigs from outside, stacking them loosely against the wall beside lengths of hazel and ash. Then, standing in the doorway, he watches the moon slip below the horizon and, for a brief time, before the sun rises, the sky is washed with red.

He had gone up to London on a drab afternoon in February, his bag heavy with Christmas presents collected from Erica Williams. Leaving the grey mass of Arundel Castle behind in the distance, it seemed as if the never-ending rows of houses, the shopping outlets and the office blocks had smothered the rolling fields of his home.

At Victoria, bag hoisted onto his shoulder, he was caught up in the milling crowds. He felt adrift, propelled by unseen hands along the platform, through the barriers, past shops and concession stands, and out across the vast expanse of the concourse. He moved relentlessly forwards, making his way to where the station clock was set high on the far side of the hall. Forwards to where James would be standing below an arch of curved stone. And James was there, his hair longer than Mike expected, wearing a blue quilted jacket that he had never seen before.

Hidden from view amongst other travellers, he saw James bend towards the girl next to him, throw an arm around her shoulder and kiss the top of her head. He realised then that James was not watching for him. Not really watching for him. Not scanning the crowds, like Mike was, with his heart pounding and excitement knotting his stomach.

It rained so much that evening. As he stared through the window all the way back to Sussex, the bag of presents on the seat beside him, drops of water hit the pane and cut trails through the dirt.

He turns back to his workbench, collects up his billhook and knives, and places them on a shelf behind the broom horse. He spreads a newspaper on the workbench, switches on the radio and, while brushing dirt from his shoes, listens to the early morning news. At the end of the broadcast, the weatherman reports that the day will be fine. In the bedroom, his suit, shrouded in a plastic cover from the dry cleaners, hangs on the wardrobe door.

From his seat in the pew, he watches his sister arrive. For a few moments, she stands in the shadow of the doorway, talking to the verger. Gracie looks serious in her dark coat, but when she spots him, smiles and raises her hand. Stepping into the aisle, she walks towards the back of the nave, her heels clicking against the flagstones.

'I stopped by for you, but you'd already left. I wasn't sure if you were coming,' she says, kissing his cheek.

'Thanks.' He opens the order of service.

Up at the front, light throws a mosaic of colour onto the chancel, and it spills across the floor. The congregation stands with a rustle, music fills church and the vicar steps to the lectern.

'I saw him outside,' she whispers. 'He walked over and thanked me for coming. Asked me to go back afterwards. Said Erica would have been pleased at the turnout. He hasn't changed much. I'd have recognised him anywhere. Older, greyer, but the same James.'

After the service, he leaves by the side door and doesn't shake hands with the man standing in the porch. It was all a long time ago. No doubt, when he pops in the shop on Saturday, he will find out if there is anything about James worth knowing. His sister is wrong, he thinks, James is heavier. His face above the stiff collar of his shirt is fleshier. Under the jacket of a dark grey suit, his body appears thicker. James looks like a man who is slow on his feet.

He walks home through the village. He stops by the pond and rolls a cigarette. The reeds by the bank have been chopped back, the stems broken, and the pond looks untidy. The water has frozen. In the middle, the ice is thick and opaque, but at the edge it is thin and clear and he can see flickers of movement in the darkness below.

In the kitchen, he peels and cores apples, the skin falling from the fruit into the washing up bowl. He arranges the slices in the base of a baking dish and sprinkles them with cloves. He works methodically, rubbing butter into sugar and flour, covering the apples with the mix and sliding the dish into the fridge. He clears the peelings away and throws them into the bin.

He will coppice more wood tomorrow if the weather is dry. He will move further into the parkland, cutting the year's birch and bringing it home to be stacked and stored until the twigs are seasoned and ready to use. Mike takes his besom from beside the rubbish bin and with broad, strong strokes, begins to sweep the floor.

A Stopping Place

THE GATE CLICKS closed behind him and the security lights, activated by his entrance, throw beams across the shadows. He catches the quick dart of a rat. Everything is as he left it. The hose is coiled above the tap, a stack of green plastic feed buckets, scrubbed clean for the morning, stand by the water trough, and an upended wheelbarrow leans against the side wall. From the stalls, he hears the scrape of metal shoes against the concrete floor and the whisper of hay nets against brickwork. His footsteps sound hollow as he crosses the yard.

Although he only turned twenty this summer, he has a manner of carrying his slight frame, a quiet way of listening, and a directness in his dark brown eyes that give him the appearance of someone older, someone to be trusted. Above all, he has a way of being with horses, an understanding of them. It's an understanding that runs deeper than muscle and bone. He's never thought about how or why. It's an innate knowledge he carries, and he accepts that it's as much a part of him as the beating of his heart.

Recommended by word of mouth, he travels from one problem animal to the next. He never stays anywhere long; a call to his mobile will see him pack his rucksack and move on. Despite these abrupt departures, his reputation as a horseman is growing and there are plenty who are happy to pass his number along.

Whilst he grew up with horses, he knows nothing about running a yard. But as far as he can see it's about working hard and learning fast. Over the last few years, there have been jobs in bigger places than this, but he likes it here, likes the informality that comes with such a small set-up. There are only two lines of boxes, three and three, joined at the right angle by a feed store and tack room. All in all, this place is ten acres of post and rail pasture tucked up tight behind the flint walls of a nineteenth century farmhouse, the whole lot perched on the shoulder of the Downs. This is the kind of place he wants to be.

His workload is light, with only two liveries to be ridden and schooled. These two hacks live alongside a retired broodmare, sway-backed and gentle, an old Shetland, and a youngster he thinks should make around thirteen hands. The last is only a child's pony and, as soon as he arrived, he turned it away for the winter. These five animals are pretty undemanding, easy doers. But in the last stall, the one furthest from the gate, there is a six-year-old gelding. A surly chestnut thoroughbred. This is the horse of his childhood dreams: a striking animal, tall and fine, with a coat that gleams in the sunlight like beaten copper. This horse is so beautifully different from the stolid piebald and skewbald cobs he grew up with. And this thoroughbred is the reason Thom is here. Although it is injured and he hasn't been able to ride him yet, Thom knows this is a horse worth hanging around for.

While he works, he sings softly under his breath, repeating the same few snatched lines he's heard in the pub. This is his favourite hour, this last check that all is well. Without fuss, he moves from stable to stable, topping up water buckets, refilling the hay and straightening the animals' rugs. He saves the thoroughbred until last and, drawing near, catches the dry rustle of straw as the animal steps from side to side, lifting one front foot then the other. Even before he slides back the bolt, he knows the horse is rocking from shoulder to shoulder, head hanging low on the arch of its neck, swaying back and forth with the regularity of a lead weight on a plumb line. His entrance stills the movement. Thom has seen this before, knows the calm is momentary, and that when he leaves the horse will begin weaving again as if led by an unseen hand.

During his first weeks on the yard, he found the gelding flighty, prone to skitting sideways when he came near. In the stable, the animal, ears flat and eyes wide with discomfort, had avoided contact, preferring to back away from him, seeking safety in the corner. Thom wasn't surprised. From what he understands, the horse has come cheap, which means it came straight from some low grade dealer. Broken-in too young. He knows how that works. Ram a bit in their mouths, throw a saddle on their backs, then get on and stay on. He's seen it. Seen horses with lather-flecked haunches, spit flying from their mouths, rearing and bucking. He's seen his uncles and cousins shouting and swearing as they hang on to ropes looped through the bridle, and seen his Da, whip in hand, lash and kick until, with its head drooping and chest heaving, the exhausted animal gives in.

In the stable, the smell of fresh urine is strong. He glances round at the banks of straw he's built against the walls, noting where he needs to skip out the damp bedding. In his pocket, his silenced mobile vibrates. He wonders if it's a text from his sister. Throughout this last week, she has begun to contact him with a daily onslaught of texts and calls. He'll deal with it later.

He reaches out and pats the horse's neck. Hello, my beauty. His voice is low and lilting. Steady, now, steady. What has Thom got here? He offers up his other hand, opening his fist at the nuzzling of the animal's lips to reveal a mint in the centre of his palm. So this is what you want? Taking his time, he glides his other hand under the rug and feels the twitch of nerves under the animal's skin. You'll live, my friend, you'll live. A couple more days, that's all we need. He feels the solid warmth of the shoulder, pushing downwards towards the flank, until he feels the rise and fall of the ribcage against his palm. With his head tilted to one side, Thom stands, counting off the seconds between each breath. In that moment, he's at one with the horse, alive to any discord, searching for heat, his fingertips seeking out the animal's pain.

Back in the flat above the garages, he toes off his boots and throws his coat over the back of the chair. The room is warm and saturated with the smell of herbs and slow-cooked meat. She's been in, the woman he works for. She must have brought the food over from the farmhouse and put it in the oven to keep warm while he was in the yard. Probably went back into her kitchen to cook the meal after they had spoken about the horse. Even laid the table, covering the scratches and heat stains in a checked cotton cloth, and left a small, round loaf on a board. Christ. She might be his boss, but this isn't part of the deal. He doesn't need anyone feeding him. All he asks is for somewhere to sleep, cash in his hand, and to be left to get on with his work. To be left alone.

With a tea towel in his hands, he carries the dinner to the table. The casserole is thick with beef and vegetables braised in red wine. It would be stupid to waste it. He cuts a piece of bread and mops the gravy. It's a bit too rich. Across the room, the television cuts to an outside broadcast, and his attention is caught by an angry voice. A man gesticulates towards a metal gate that's been lifted from its hinges and, he claims, flung into the hedge. Thom finishes his meal listening to a reporter churning out the same spiel he has heard before.

The reporter drones on about trespass and eviction. There are questions regarding expected clean-up costs and a discussion with the local councillor about when the travellers could be moved to a permanent site. At the end of the item, the camera pans across a tyre-rutted field, lingering over piles of rubbish, a couple of sofas and, to finish, an old car balanced on bricks. In the background, a collection of caravans are parked up with their doors shut. Mostly six berthers, the vans are massed around a central clearing. Thom looks hard at the largest one, taking in the navy stripe down the side and the open blinds. He imagines the face of a child at the window.

Earlier, as he sat on an old wooden bench at the back of the tack room working leather soap into the pommel of a saddle, he'd been thinking of the messages collecting on his phone. Thinking of his sister, thinking that he might have to go back, he didn't hear anyone cross the yard. It caught him unawares. The sound of her voice speaking his name had thrown him and, when he looked up, he half expected to see his sister standing in the doorway and not the woman he worked for.

All I wanted to know, she said, was how the gelding was getting on. He told her that the heat from the foreleg had gone. The horse would be fine now. He was blunt with her. Don't push him. Give him time. He needs gentle handling. Perhaps his words were overly sharp – he didn't think so – but she stepped backwards saying she didn't want to argue with him. In her opinion, she said, the horse wasn't fine. After all, he wasn't sound enough to ride yet. Although he didn't tell her, Thom knows this is true, but it is only a case of building him up and gaining his confidence. You must bring him back slowly that's all, he told her. And really, she didn't need him to do that. He thought the conversation was over, had just reached out for the tin of soap when she spoke again. Are you thinking of leaving, Thom? Remember, you agreed to stay until the horse was completely sound. That was what annoyed him. It wasn't as if he needed reminding of their agreement. Yes, she was right, but things change, he wanted to say. He was pleased when she turned to leave and began rubbing soap on his cloth not realising she'd stopped at the door. I was told you were a man of your word, she said. After she left, the sentence hung in the air around him.

Plate to one side, he reads through his messages. According to his sister, Ma is worse and is asking for him. Please come, his sister says. You have to come, Thom. Ma's in hospital and she wants you. Hospital? Ma should be in a hospice, that's for sure; probably should have gone into one weeks ago. No doubt it was left too late. That would be Da's doing, keeping to the old ways. Da, some kind of man he is with his stupid blind ignorance, like some throwback to the 50s, always shouting the odds and always quick with his fists to make his point.

He should phone his sister. He pops the cap from a bottle of beer, leans back in his chair and watches the television.

~

The bus stops and he sees the men, a milling crowd of about twenty, gathered in front of the building. Behind them, a mix of dirty vans, twin cabs and new Jeeps are blocking the disabled parking spaces. They've come in force. There are enough chrome horseshoes fixed to over-large fenders to tell him that. Even from this distance, he can make out the broad shoulders and black hair of his Da as he steps out of the Jeep, and the swagger of his two younger brothers, baggy and loose-limbed in denim. Through the dirty window of the bus shelter, he watches them slam the doors, cross the road and join the others.

It's obvious they would be here. Yet, seeing them all together like this makes his stomach clench. He takes a moment, bending down to retie his laces. His mobile rings. For Christ's sake, it's the yard again. Why is he not surprised? He has already told her the gelding will be okay, that she will be riding him soon. He hesitates. How many times does he have say, be patient? He turns the phone off and makes his way towards the group outside the hospital.

One by one, the men fall silent as he draws level. He can feel their attention shifting back and forth from his Da to himself. His youngest brother, hands in the pockets of his hoodie, steps into his path. The boy is close, close enough for Thom to smell a flat, stale odour on his breath. None of us wants you here, he tells Thom. Da said if anyone was to call you, there would be trouble. That's about right. Da dealing out the smacks and punches. Without a word to Thom, his Da reaches out, grabs the teenager's arm and drags him away. Leave it, son, he tells the boy. Thom steps off the curb and walks into the road to pass them. His pace is measured. He looks forward and focuses on the entrance straight ahead.

Inside, it's bright and warm. Too warm. He smells food, cooked, cooking, he's not sure. He's in a reception area with a desk and rows of orange plastic seats, all empty. A vending machine stands in the corner and a couple of wheelchairs are set to one side. Signs on the walls, corridors lead off to his right and left. Pathology. Histology. Oncology. Paediatrics. Each department is colour-coded. In the distance, the sound of footsteps, voices and a shout of laughter. He stops for a moment, then turns to follow the blue dots painted on the floor.

He sits beside her, listening to the rattle of her breathing, watching her eyes flick back and forth beneath her closed lids. The curtains are drawn around her bed, shutting them away from the comings and goings of the ward. He leans in to kiss her, the sweet, musky smell he noticed when he arrived at her bedside still stronger near her body. Her skin is jaundiced and tight across her cheekbones. A catheter runs from under the bedclothes, draining her urine into a bag.

He loses all sense of time. How long had it been since he'd been at the stables, turning the gelding out into a field while he cleaned the stall, the morning alive with the perfume of fresh straw. He had drunk his coffee leaning against the gate, watching the horse crop at the grass, checking for lameness as the animal moved from patch to patch. He straightens his Ma's pillow and smooths the bedclothes, tucking them under the mattress. The rise of her rib-cage is held fast beneath the sheet. She is thin, thinner than he wants her to be.

The nurses have told him to talk to her; she can hear him. At first, he stumbles over his words, wondering what to say to her, offering her sentences at random. And then, as he sits beside her with the gentle pressure of his hand on her arm, he is her boy again and the words are easy. Couldn't wait to get away, could I, he says. And it's a funny thing, he tells her, these punters, they are all the same, all cut from the same cloth. They phone, they say they really need me, tell me the horses need me, yet when I get there it's a kitchen with a butler's sink, a dresser loaded with china and a bloody Aga for them, and some shitty flat above the stables for me. No surprise there, Ma.

As he talks, he no longer notices passing footsteps, the rustle of clothing or the murmur of voices on the other side of the curtains. He says he is thinking about settling down. It's about time. There might be a place coming up on a new yard, bringing an eventer back from injury and breaking in some youngsters. Y'know how it is Ma, I've always wanted to be some place permanent. Have always wanted to find my stopping place. Remember that winter site, down Littlehampton way – couldn't wait for us to pitch up there, could I? Couldn't wait to get to school for a few months. And Da throwing my books out of the van into the rain. Bastard.

You do remember, don't you, Ma? Maybe this job will be my chance. I'll give them a call later and let you know.

When he can no longer see the rise and fall of her chest, he leans forward and takes her hand in his.

I'm not unhappy, Ma, he tells her.

Outside, the familiar sweet smell of tobacco from their rollies surrounds him. With a shuffling of feet, they part to let him through. At first glance, his Da seems the same, but close up he notices the greying hair at his temples, the lines on his forehead and a thickening round his waist. You're a fucking bastard, Thom tells him. A bastard and a bully. It's been four years since Thom's seen him, and this time it's his Da who looks away first.

The cloud has cleared. Any warmth from the day has leached away, and now, a short while after sunset, there's frost in the air. In the coming hours, it will only get colder. Thom tucks the ends of his scarf under his collar and zips his jacket up tight. There's a cold wind now. It gusts across the car park, stinging his face and making his eyes water. With it comes a faint smell of the distant sea. He glances up to the disc of the moon rising above the red tiled roof of the hospital and smiles. It's a poacher's moon, full and bold. He feels the lure of it in the pit of his stomach.

He swings his rucksack up onto his shoulders and, turning his phone back on, strides out towards the bus stop. As he walks, he listens to his voicemail. By rights, he should forget any new job and go back to the yard. He has yet to ride the gelding, and he wants that. He wants to sit in the saddle, his legs against the horse, feeling the stretch down his calf and the pressure of the stirrup on his foot. He wants to feel the shift of the horse, the pull of muscle against bone. The swift, easy movement as they canter across the grass. The two of them. Thom and the horse. It will be their moment; a fine moment. And he is certain, he will never have felt quite this free before.

Chichester and Arundel

A Friend of the Gallery

THE OIL WAS small, a nude woman, cross-legged on the edge of a rumpled bed, her chin resting on her hand, her face in profile. She was held captive by the edges of the canvas, the extravagant full curves of her body trapped in the moment as she gazed away into the depths of the painting towards the shadows, where, in strokes of blue and grey, a man leant, arms folded, over the back of a chair.

Kathy had discovered the painting as she wandered through the gallery, away from the stark, white of the modern extension, past the panelling and fireplaces in the old house, and up to the first-floor rooms. At the time, she felt the picture was overshadowed by larger pieces, but on days when the building was cool and peaceful, and footsteps and voices muted, it drew her. Through stone-floored hallways and high-ceilinged stairwells, away from the Blakes and Burras, the Moores and the Nicholsons, the painting drew her straight past all the other exhibits in the gallery's collection.

Every time she looked at it, every time she sought the picture out, Kathy found herself attracted to the bold arch of the woman's legs, the flush of her skin and the dark smudge of her nipple. *Walter Richard Sickert 1860 – 1942 Jack Ashore c. 1912.*

It was a while back, on their twenty-fifth wedding anniversary, that her husband had decided they should both become Friends of the Gallery. She was sitting on the sofa and he, ankles crossed, in the armchair opposite. He smiled when he handed her the membership card with her name, Mrs Kathy Richards, in script across the front. He said it would be good to have a nice hobby to broaden their interests as they got older; give them something to discuss, stop them becoming stale. While he spoke, she stared at the pallid gap of flesh between his sock and his trousers. Was she getting old? Had she had her life and this was all there was to look forward to? A nice hobby. She stared at his fish-belly white leg as if she had never seen it before, and didn't reply. Over the next few weeks, his words dropped into her mind when she least expected them, disturbing her, like stones kicked into water.

One evening, when the membership was still fresh, they had attended a preview at the gallery. *Artists' Studies: From Pencil to Paint.* Drinks and a talk in the company of like-minded people, her husband told her, helping her on with her coat. It would be interesting, he went on; they were, after all, Friends of one of the country's most important galleries for British modern art. And it was right on their doorstep. No dragging up to the city for them. Weren't they lucky? She didn't feel lucky. More than likely, she would be bored. Yet, whilst the atmosphere of evening struck her as false and the chatter of the Friends annoying, when Kathy stood at the back of the room, a glass of warm wine in her hand, she found herself listening. The talk was enjoyable. Mulling this over as they drove home through the dark streets, she decided her husband had been right. Perhaps it would be interesting to visit the gallery again.

Kathy never told her husband about her visits to the gallery, never mentioned discovering *Jack Ashore* and never talked about her fascination with Sickert's painting. Not once had she considered asking him for his views. One warm afternoon, he caught her settled in the garden, a book about Modernism open on her lap. He was pleased to see her taking an interest in art, he told her, and looking at the book over her shoulder, offered little insights he was sure she would find helpful. Had she other books like this? She shook her head. Never mind, he would look out for some. Nothing too difficult. Fine, she said, leaving the book on the grass. Kathy would never let him catch her like this again.

She bought a tablet and, keeping it fully charged, tucked it out of sight down the side of her bag. After some practice, it was easy to use. When alone, she enjoyed slipping it from the case and flitting back and forth from website to website. She began to develop a skill for finding the right places, the right forums. For finding others who shared a similar interest. And all the time, she moved further through the web. The deeper she went, the more discussions she found, and the more discussions she found, the more fragments she gathered of Sickert's life. She only had to read about him, or see images of his paintings, for the artist to lift from the screen and become vivid and alive in her mind. His time in France and Italy, his marriages, his illegitimate son; these things stole into her thoughts until, bit by bit, she felt herself falling into the artist's world.

Sometimes, digging in her garden amongst the smells of damp earth and wet leaves, Kathy found she was thinking of Sickert searching for models on the waterfront in Venice. And once, emerging from the gym into the dark evening, she glimpsed a hurrying figure reflected in a shop window and imagined a girl, long-skirted, her hair tucked into a bonnet, caught in the pooling glow of a streetlamp. She pictured her leaving the artist's studio, rushing home in the half light, the heels of her boots tapping against the pavement and marking her journey through the dark back alleyways of a drab Camden Town.

Kathy wanted to know more. She was missing something, and felt it was lingering on the outskirts of her reach. Perhaps it was necessary to see other pieces of Sickert's work in the same way she saw *Jack Ashore*. In the flesh. With this on her mind, she planned a trip, telling her husband it was a girls' day out. Shopping and lunch, she said. She hurried from Victoria Station through the streets of Pimlico towards the Thames and the towering columns of Tate Britain. In the rooms of this much larger gallery, with the hum of other visitors for company, she studied the Sickerts, moving slowly from picture to picture. Standing in front of the portraits and nature studies, she realised that these early pieces held no interest for her. This wasn't the Sickert she longed to see. She liked his darker canvasses, the music hall and theatre scenes. These were the paintings that excited her.

Sitting at home, her tablet on her lap, she concentrated her research on this time in the artist's life. Gradually, she began to understand the paintings. She began to understand the risks he took with his work. The more she learnt as she searched online, the more she became fascinated with the tawdry existence created in the dark, gloomy tones of the stark interiors and the creamy skin of the nudes. But, most of all, it was *Jack Ashore* that she began to understand. The piece held her captive. This was her painting.

Funny, she had never believed in fate. She had no time for mysterious intervention. All such notions were nonsense. No, life was made up of facts, straightforward facts. She'd met her husband because they worked for the same company. Simple as that. They chatted, went out for meals and visited the cinema. He was steady, considered a good catch by everyone, and she had not hesitated when he asked her to marry him. Then, the years had rolled past for the two of them rattling around in their over-large house. Under different circumstances, she would have met and married somebody else, and they would have had different holidays, made other friends. Perhaps they would have had children. She'd never doubted the facts and, whatever else their life together was, she was certain it was nothing to do with fate.

Yet, looking back over the last few months made her question this. Later, she would say to herself that she couldn't believe what had happened. It began with the slam of the front door as her husband left for work. She remembered settling down in the armchair, her tablet in front of her, using the time to research Sickert's mistresses. From 'nude models' to 'painted ladies' to 'art lovers', she flicked through the links. Kathy would later tell herself it was strange that she had managed to type just the right combination of words to bring up a link to the chat room 'IllicitEncounters'. No matter what happened, she was certain it was something she would never understand. Yes, it was finding this site that made her wonder. Surely then, this must be fate.

At first, she hung back on the edge of the chat room, reading threads, skipping from group to group, from conversation to conversation, not quite believing that all she had to do was introduce herself to become a part of this internet world. She set up a new email address. If she was ever tempted to get involved, she would not make up a ridiculous identity, could not begin to see herself as a 'LegsEleven' or a 'CuddlePuss'. But it was ridiculous thinking like this. She would never consider joining in.

Hi, I'm Kate1912.

She hit return.

It was easier than Kathy could have imagined.

~

As she stood before her painting, Kathy felt closer to Sickert than ever before. She wondered about the woman on the bed. Perhaps she was one of his wives or, most likely, a prostitute, glad to earn her money as an artist's model. She considered, not for the first time, what it would be like to sit for him hour after hour. Naked. The two of them. In one room. Artist and model. A shiver ran down her spine as she stared at the picture and she folded her arms across her chest, feeling the soft wool of her jacket under her fingers. She heard people approaching, voices coming closer, and left her place in front of the oil to make her way down through the gallery to the café.

It was crowded when she walked in, busy with the smells of toast and coffee, the clink of cutlery on china, and the bright chatter of eager conversations. She sat at a table beside the large sliding doors and scanned the room for faces she might know. Another Friend perhaps, another one of those boring stalwarts she had seen at the exhibitions, another like her husband, who moved from group to group, wine glass and canapé in hand, so very pleased with themselves.

Outside in the courtyard, tables were set beneath lantern-strung trees. She'd seen how magical it looked as dusk fell on a summer's evening, but at this moment, in the daylight, it all seemed rather bare. At a bird feeder, blue tits pecked at peanuts, their movements quick and sharp. There was a flash of red as a robin tried to join them, but they pushed the intruder away in a flurry of wings and racing heartbeats.

She looked at her reflection in the café's sliding doors: a woman with a slight smile and her hair swept back in a tortoiseshell Alice band, mid-forties but, hopefully, looking young for her age. Her dark curls were soft against her off-white polo neck. No one knew where she was and, to be honest, who would she tell. She ordered a coffee.

The night before, she'd woken with a jolt, a knot of anxiety deep in her stomach. She lay on her back staring into the dark, listening to the rhythm of her husband's breathing. What if she was recognised when she was in the café? Or what if her car was spotted while parked in the car park? Would it matter? No, she was only having lunch. Everything would be okay. Everything was organised. The hotel was booked, the lunch date arranged and, above all, there was still time to back out. She would take care. She turned on her side, adjusted the duvet around her shoulders and closed her eyes.

Now, with less than half an hour to go, the night-time doubts resurfaced. She should leave. How stupid, she should never have arranged to meet up. She stared into the courtyard. What if, by another quirk of fate, she realised when he walked towards her that she already knew him? No photos, that's what she'd said. She wanted nothing like that arriving in her inbox. Well, what would she do? Smile and say 'hello', as though the whole incident were a chance meeting? She could act as if the person she was waiting for had yet to arrive. Maybe even mention that they were late. It was a case of holding her nerve.

Of course, Kathy wondered what he looked like: tall and bald, short and stocky, dark or fair. In her thoughts, he was indistinct, never fully imagined, always remaining out of reach. Across the café, a man hesitated in the open doorway, glanced around, and made his way towards her.

'Kate?' he asked, holding out his hand.

He was tallish, fortyish, with brown hair, a blue shirt and beige chinos. Inside her head, a voice – her voice – told her to look puzzled, to tell him that he was mistaken, she was sorry but she was waiting for a friend.

'You are Kate, aren't you? You said dark hair and white jumper, sitting at a table by the patio doors. I'm not making a total idiot of myself, am I?'

His hand was large and she could feel his warmth as she shook it. The skin on the edge of his thumb was smooth against her palm.

'No. I mean, yes. I'm Kate,' she replied.

Over lunch, they chatted, their conversation light, effortless and full of good humour. She talked about the delicate gilded porcelain in the cabinets upstairs, each piece covered in hand-painted flowers. She told him she liked the heavy brown furniture, the intricate inlay on the marquetry chests and the hand-carved chairs that could be found dotted around the rooms.

'Are you local? I thought you must be. I mean, you never said anything, but I wondered why you chose to meet here,' he said.

'No, not at all. I was early and had a look round,' she said, signalling to the waitress for the bill. 'Don't you think we should go now?'

'Shame. I hoped you might show me the place. Like you said, it's interesting here.' He laughed. 'Unless, of course, you have other plans.' He was still smiling as he studied the bill. 'Right, let's see the damage.'

She watched as he scanned down the items.

'Twenty five quid each. That leaves a tip. Okay?'

She'd thought to bring cash.

~

She lay still, careful not to touch him, her arms outside the covers pinning the cotton sheet across her naked body. With the curtains closed, the room was cool and dim. Resting there, all she thought about were the colours in the room, the white of the walls, the grey synthetic carpet, grey and red curtains, and the fake oak wardrobe. In the corner, his shirt and her jumper had fallen from the chair and were a tangled mess on the floor. She hoped he was asleep. Without looking at him, she slid her legs from the bed and sat on the edge. He didn't speak.

In the bath, she rested her head on a folded towel and let the water wash away the woody smell of his aftershave and the sweet, musky scent of their sex. Her limbs felt heavy, lethargic in the heat. Her thoughts were full of disconnected images: her husband mowing the grass, two white china mugs next to a kettle, an open window with net curtains catching in the breeze. She remembered how earlier, when she arrived at the gallery, a group of lads were gathered on the pavement, uniformed in skin tight jeans and bomber jackets. They fell silent as she passed. She remembered how their collective gaze crawled across her, how closely her fitted jacket enclosed her breasts, and how she'd looked straight ahead. And she remembered their adolescent laughter exploding behind her as she entered the building.

With a towel wrapped around her body, she gathered up her clothes.

He was awake, propped up, his shoulders resting on the wooden headboard, the sheet pushed away from his body. He seemed over-large in the dim-light, his bulky frame filling the bed. She returned to the bathroom to dress. In her hurry, she snagged a fingernail on the clasp of her bra. Her hair had curled in the damp and she ran her fingers through the unruly strands.

'Goodbye,' she said, taking her handbag from beside the bed.

At the door, she paused. He didn't offer her money towards the cost of the room. She didn't ask for any.

As she drove through the afternoon traffic, she heard the cathedral clock chime five. She stopped at the shop on the corner and bought salad leaves and mushrooms. At home, she opened a bottle of red wine and cooked rib-eye steak for supper, filling the kitchen with the smell of seared fat. While the mushrooms spat in the hot oil, her husband poured the wine. She looked up from setting the table and, with her hands full of cutlery, told him about visiting the gallery. She was there for such a long time, she said. Did he know they had a painting by Walter Sickert called *Jack Ashore*?

For the first time, she spoke to him about Sickert's nude. She rolled the stem of her wine glass between her fingers, remarking on the detail and the intensity in the colours, pointing out the artist's use of brush work in the rumpled bed covers. She talked about the soft tones of the nude's skin, mentioned the way her dark hair was pinned up away from her neck, the hint of shadows across the slope of her shoulders, and the play of light and shade. It was a complicated piece. She mentioned how the woman looked back into the room, face angled, with a slight curve to her lips. Yet she didn't mention, not now, not ever, how the trace of the woman's smile was masked in the cup of her hand.

Prey

THE DEATH LAST night had been good, calm and easy, and although she feels weary, there is always, at the end, the sense of a job well done. It was Edna's time, they both knew that, and she had been there to help her on her way.

After spending all night in Edna's over-warm room, the day feels clean and sharp. The April sun is high and, despite a hint of diesel fumes from the first few early buses, the morning air refreshes her. Takeaway coffee and Danish pastry in hand, she crosses the cathedral green, her footsteps leaving prints on the damp grass.

She pauses at a bench, wipes away the beads of dew, and settles down to watch the flow of people hurrying past: office workers, shop assistants, a man dragging a wheelie bin, and a group of uniformed school girls, giggling and chatting as they get off a bus. She's hungry. It's odd how hungry a death makes her. She never expected that. Nor had she expected to feel so in tune with her own body after each passing – to feel so concentrated. The pastry is still warm. She leans back, picks off the caramelised pecans one by one and pops them in her mouth, relishing the taste, bitter-sweet like cinder toffee, across her tongue.

Above her, high in the turrets around the spire, a pair of peregrine have built a nest. She looks up, squinting against the sun, to see if she can catch sight of them perched amongst the ledges. Every spring, the birds return to lay their eggs and rear their young. A few years back, when she was new to the area, she'd spent an afternoon on the green, watching the birds through binoculars. She spotted them as they flew back and forth, recognising the black flash of their heads against the grey of the stone. She'd been in luck and her persistence was rewarded with a sighting of the female resting high on the building, clutching the limp body of a kill in the talons on its strong, yellow feet. She licks the last of the pastry's sticky, maple filling from her fingers and drinks the dregs of her coffee.

Everything about Edna's final moments had gone to plan, and she is glad about that. The old lady had met the occasion with true dignity, hadn't struggled or railed against it. 'Go in peace,' she said to her, speaking the words that released Edna's soul on its journey home. As usual, it's the thoughtful little touches she provides before the end that turn the whole affair into a special occasion. In Edna's case, she'd placed a talisman in the old woman's palm, curling her frail fingers around the pink gemstone to keep it close. This, she told her, would bring comfort against the darkness closing in. To bring peace and restore harmony, she filled an oil burner with rose oil, and then, as the perfume of a summer garden infused the room, she lit, as she always did, a twin-flamed candle for guidance.

There's no sign of the peregrine; all she can see are a couple of gulls adorning a gargoyle. The shops are open, the day becoming busier and nosier. In her bag is the money she's taken from Edna's bedside cabinet. It needs banking before she does anything else. The sunshine has no real warmth in it and she knows she should make her way home before she gets too cold. She gathers her rubbish, pushing the empty wrapper into the paper cup, but doesn't get up. Her bones feel heavy, the initial sense of elation has left her and she is drained. She closes her eyes for a minute or two, leans back against the bench once more, and lets her attention wander. Sounds rise and fall: birdsong, footsteps, traffic, snatches of conversation, traffic and, above it all, the deep tones of the cathedral bell striking the hour.

When she thinks about it, she really does have a difficult job. Challenging. On the surface, it must seem strange to others. The idea of sitting next to a bed and holding the hand of the dying could possibly seem unnerving. And yet, for her, this isn't true. It's peaceful, she tells them, when she is pressed into a discussion. Of course, she does have confidentiality boundaries and there are things said between her client and herself, personal things, that she would never reveal. The dying often ramble, as happened with her mother. Pain relief can make them do that. But, at the end, it comes down to two things, maybe three: forgiveness, absolution and retribution. Yes, sometimes people need retribution.

To assist in a tranquil and gentle death, this is what she does. This is what she's needed for. She's present at the bedside to provide a healing space, a sacred space. No, she's never been frightened. Why would she be? Her duty is to take away fear, not to feel it. To smooth the path for her clients and make certain that there is nothing for them to be frightened of. Isn't that the kind of passing we would all like for our loved ones? And ourselves?

Her clients, although she likes to call them 'friends', have, as a rule, asked her to be there and, hand in hand, they set out to journey across a spiritual threshold, which, make no mistake, is an absorbing process. In those final hours, she finds most people are seeking to be at peace. Closure, that's what most of them want.

She sees her work as a vocation, a calling rather than a job. It's hard work. And yes, of course, being a soul midwife is not for everyone. For her, it had been an obvious choice; she had first-hand experience, if you count all those hours sitting by the bed when her mother was dying. She even gave up her job at the building society so she could nurse her at home. It was the least she could do for her mum. Following the funeral, things changed; she changed. She felt at a loose end, as if floating away from her old life. After a lot of thought, she sold her mother's house and decided to rent for a while. She booked onto a training course. It turned out that for her, helping people die was a fresh start.

Nearby a car horn sounds. The sudden blast disturbs her and she opens her eyes.

At home, in her townhouse overlooking the canal, she lays her bag on the worktop and moves with purpose, opening curtains and fanlights, filling the rooms with light and the faint earthy smell of slow moving water. The décor is all her own. Plain ivory coloured walls, oatmeal carpet and light oak furniture. Everything new; she'd taken nothing from her mother's. The year she turned fifty, she bought the house outright, paying with the money she'd earned. She thought of it as a present, a parting gift from her clients.

Back in the kitchen, she empties a sachet of porridge into a bowl, measures out milk and pops it all into the microwave. She eats at the table on her balcony, looking at the patterns of sunlight shifting on the surface of the water. She has been busy these last few months, that's for sure, and there's been no time to look after herself. Whilst she doesn't bother a great deal about her appearance, she would be the first to admit her short hair is in need of a colour and a cut. Her work can be all consuming, but she doesn't mind. Not one bit. She's very serious about her clients. And that's the truth. She places her dirty china in the dishwasher, then washes the sickly, lingering essence of rose oil from her skin.

The room is chilled. A sudden gust billows the curtains, the squall battering the windows with heavy drops of rain. Shouts of surprise carry through the open window and, when she glances out, a group of visitors are hurrying to board a waiting barge. She watches, tired yet glad to be here, in her own home, enjoying all the commotion outside, taking pleasure in the bustle as one by one people are helped aboard the rocking boat.

Much of her work is carried out during the night. This is when she's needed to keep a vigil. This is when the hours seem longest, when the friends and family have gone, when nothing else matters and, in the soft glow of the candles, questions can be asked about what might happen, about what might be waiting on the other side. And because this is when she's needed, she dresses, re-packs her bag and, locking the front door, walks away from her house by the water through the early evening streets, back towards the city.

The hospice is quiet when she arrives. Rubber-soled footsteps are muted against the vinyl, voices mutter behind closed doors and even the ringing phone sounds distant. The door to Edna's room is open. It's been cleaned ready for the next patient, a weak smell of antiseptic and sanitiser lingering in the air. The bed has been stripped and fresh bedding, laundered and folded, is piled on a chair.

In the office, she checks the admissions with the duty nurse and finds that her next client is not expected until tomorrow.

'Shame you've had a wasted journey,' the nurse says. 'We've taken in one new one. He's got a while yet, I'd say, but who can tell. We're a bit short-staffed tonight and there's no family or friends around – any chance you could sit with him for a bit, as you're here?' The nurse is smiling as she flicks the switch on the kettle. 'He's upstairs, room five. Name's Michael. Here are his notes; have a quick read while I make you a cup of tea to take up with you.'

'Go on, then,' she says.

'It needn't be for long,' the nurse says, pouring hot water in to a mug.

This time, she'll sit for a while as a volunteer. There will be no money to collect. He has no one to leave a cheque for her. This time there won't be a fee to bank. But it isn't about the money, she doesn't need it, her house is paid for and she has enough saved. Once or twice, she's found herself explaining this, without any personal details, to some of the families who contact her. Those who can afford it do pay her, after all she is a professional, she tells them. And others, like now, well, that's a different story. She opens the file and begins to read.

Saunders: Michael. Seventy-six years old.

This isn't right. It can't be. She reads the page again. Michael Saunders. Never. Not that Michael Saunders. Bound to be more than one man with the same name. This is a coincidence. Or a joke. Yes, it has to be some kind of joke, a spiteful trick designed to unnerve her. But if so, who's in on it? Who's making fun of her? Not the people at the care home. No, they hardly know her. Perhaps it's here, at the hospice?

'You don't take sugar, do you?' the nurse says, passing her the cup. 'Everything okay? You look bothered. Not a problem with the paperwork?'

'No, I'm just being silly. A coincidence, that's all.' She checks the file. Is it the same man? No, can't be. 'Same name as a friend of my mum's. It caught me by surprise. Over forty-odd years ago, when I was growing up. Still caught me off guard though.' She looks towards the nurse. 'We lost touch. Anyway, it can't be him. Can it?'

'Well, he's not originally from round here, relocated quite a while back. As I mentioned, no family noted.' The nurse takes the file and places it on the desk. 'Been going on a bit, most of it nonsense, you know how it is, but he's stopped all that now. You alright to sit with him?'

'Yes. Yes, it's what I do. I'll be fine.'

'Great. I'll pop up later and see how he's doing.'

'Back then, when I was a little girl, I called him Uncle Mick,' she says, taking her cup.

Room five is at the front of the house. She'd visited a client here once before. It's pleasant, small, square, in shades of cream and sage, with an outlook to the east over the garden and, further away, above the neighbouring rooftops towards the grey spire of the cathedral.

'Hello, Michael,' she says as she enters. 'I've come to sit with you for a while if you'd like that.'

At the sound of her voice, the man turns his head. He is hollowed-cheeked, his skin waxen. She closes the door and moves towards the bed. The nurse is right, it isn't his time tonight. He'll last another day, maybe even two.

She looks for features she might recognise. Her fingers are clasped round the handle of the mug. She can feel the heat from the tea against her knuckles. On the pillow, his hair looks thick and dark, and yet, as she steps nearer, she can see it is over-long and streaked with grey. His eyes are rheumy and puddle-water brown. Around him hangs the sour odour of his weakening body.

The room is quiet, and she thinks she can hear the beat of her heart above the rasp of his breathing.

Drink in hand, she moves to the window. The earlier squalls have stopped and, in the garden, a woman works amongst the shrubs, her blond head bobbing to the rhythm of her digging, the ends of her pink scarf catching in the wind. It could be him. She watches while the woman gathers up her gardening tools and moves away, disappearing from sight behind a shed. Yes, it could be him. She looks towards the cathedral and wonders if there is any chance she can see the peregrine from this distance. At best, she hopes to make out the birds on the soar by the broad, pointed span of their outstretched wings as they glide around the spire.

Her tea has gone cold. She places the cup on the bedside cabinet next to a small CD player and brings a chair close to the bed.

'Michael. It's me. Lillian. You remember me, don't you? Bella's girl. You called me Lily.' She leans in close. 'Remember? Your little Lily.'

His hands move on top of the covers. She catches a sigh and the faint scratch of his nails against cotton as his thumbs and index fingers pluck at the sheet.

'And you were my Uncle Mick,' she says, with a smile.

She takes her oil burner from her bag. 'In a minute, I'll prepare the room, make it comfortable, because I am staying with you. Just for a bit. We'll be able to talk about old times,' she says, patting his arm. 'That'll be nice, won't it?' She glances at the bed. His eyes have closed and a thin line of spit runs from the corner of his mouth.

'Spikenard oil. We'll have spikenard oil. I've never felt the need to use it at a passing before. It has a funny aroma, bitter. You might find it unpleasant. Some people do, but I don't mind it,' she says, adding a few drops to the burner. 'A useful oil. Good for soul wounds. Helps with remembering, and it can sometimes trigger flashbacks.'

She lights a vigil candle and places it on the cabinet, the flame fluttering in a draft.

'Such a long time ago, Uncle Mick. So many memories. Where shall we start? That cottage in Cornwall? What was I then? Ten? You made Mum take me out of school for that holiday. So many treats, I thought we'd gone to Paradise. We'd never had it so good. And Mum never stopped laughing.'

She reaches out, takes his hand and squeezes his fingers, pinching them hard against her own. 'There, I expect it's all coming back to you.' His bones are fragile in her grip. She catches hold of his other hand.

'This is nice. Let's have some more candles. You'd like that, wouldn't you? And while they burn, we can have more of a chat. I don't know what you believe. Heaven and hell? Karma? Afterlife? What do you imagine is waiting for you when it's all over? Don't you worry, it will soon be over. All the pain, gone. Trust me, Uncle Mick, everything comes to an end.'

She releases his hands and watches as they begin, once more, to worry at the sheet.

'Mum's laughing didn't last, did it? Soon turned to shouting, and then to tears.'

The click of her lighter is loud as, one by one, she lights the candles.

'Really, we'd been fine on our own, you know, Mum and me, before you came along.' She turns to face him. 'When I was older, I realised it was all about the money. When that ran out, so did you.'

Michael's hands still. A tear seeps from his closed eyes, follows the beak of his nose and is lost on the pillow.

'And we never knew where you went. Must have been planning your escape for a while. Wardrobe emptied, shaving stuff packed, every bit of you gone. Mum's jewellery box. Gone. The money in my piggy bank. Gone. Now you're leaving again. Funny how things turn out,' she says, moving to the window sill. 'We must take care, the nurses pop in to check everything's okay, and one thing they don't like is candles up here. Too dangerous. Health and safety. You understand, Uncle Mick. But until they look in, we can do whatever we like. Who's to know? I won't tell if you won't. It'll be our little secret.' And she moves around placing the candles, the lights reflecting in the window, in the plastic water jug and across the walls, until the room is full of tiny flames.

'It was the horses, wasn't it?' She sits, edging the chair closer to the bed, and takes his hand again. 'There, doesn't this room look wonderful? Oh, you're moved. Don't be. I always make an effort to make everything comfortable. It's what I do. Why I'm here. To help you have a peaceful departure from this life.' She takes a tissue and wipes away another tear from his cheek. 'Always the horses with you. Choose a horse, Lily, you'd say. Whichever one you want. You're my lucky charm. Today's the day, Lily, I can feel it. And then it wasn't your fault when they lost, was it? Never your fault when it all went wrong. Luck always against you. Fates conspiring. But you're lucky now, Uncle Mick. It was luck that brought you here, so we could find each other again and spend this time together. Shall we have some music?'

The snap as she inserts the disk in the player makes him flinch, his head jerking against the pillow.

'You must have known that we'd lose everything after you left,' she says, as the room fills with the gentle murmur of moving water, the ebb and flow of waves across shingle.

At the window, she looks out onto the darkening garden and wonders what time the first star will appear. In her mind's eye, she sees a young Michael Saunders, mid-thirties, in shirt sleeves, jacket on the back of the chair, cigarette in an ashtray, newspaper spread on the table, betting slips and pencil.

'Mum always worrying. The debts, that's what did it. Worked all hours to try and pay them back,' she says, without turning. 'Some would say it was a long time ago. Water under the bridge. Best to let it rest. But people should be held to account. You would agree with that, wouldn't you?'

She moves back to the bed, places a hand on his forehead and strokes his hair. It's hard to know for sure if it's him. He is still. His skin is cold and his breathing shallow. He yawns as his body struggles to draw in air, yet she knows it's not his time. Experience tells her he could last another couple of days. From the jug, she tips water onto a sponge and moistens his lips. She takes a spare pillow from the chair.

'Don't be scared,' she says, leaning over the bed. 'Here, let me make you more comfortable.'

After she has blown out the candles and packed her bag, she stands once more at the side of the bed, looking at the face resting on the pillow. With care, she closes his eyes and straightens his arms outside the covers, laying his hands palms down. Her vigil over, the room and the body tidy, she makes her way through the quiet corridors back to the office. Here she fills out the necessary paperwork with the nurse and waits to speak with the duty doctor.

The morning sky is streaked red when she leaves the hospice. It's chilly outside, and damp with the promise of rain. She sees no one as she walks through the streets into the centre of the city. She crosses the green, stops by her bench, and looks up at the cathedral. High on the turret, she thinks she can make out the shape of a bird, crouched, dark against the grey stone and, as the sun rises, sees she is right. She waits, a small, quiet woman gripping the back of the bench, until the peregrine leaves its perch and wheels up into the sky. Strong and powerful, it circles the spire before plummeting earthwards in pursuit of its prey.

Undercurrents

SHE WAS GLAD to reach the towpath at the top of the embankment. Up here, the cold breeze stung her cheeks. It caught her hair and tugged it back from her face. She could see across the fields to the railway track, and beyond to the flash of vehicles on the bypass. She turned downriver towards the distant coast and, for a second, thought she could taste the air, salty on her tongue.

That afternoon, she walked straight through town from the surgery, crossed the bridge, and decided to cut through the fields to the place where the river looped through the floodplain. The grey walls of Arundel Castle towered above her as she made her way down Mill Road. She shivered in the shadows.

Her shoes were thin-soled, made for pavements and not for a track such as this, rutted and littered with stones. She made her way with care in case she twisted her ankle. How silly to come in this direction, but she hadn't felt up to bumping into people she knew and exchanging pleasantries. Not yet. Not until she could answer in a steady voice, 'I'm good. How are you?'

The Arun was low; the tide running out to the sea. She stared into the currents as they twisted through the broken bones of an old pontoon, watching a plastic bottle spin in the eddies around the upright posts. On the rising wind, she caught the dank smell of mud from the exposed banks and, from overhead, heard the beat of wings as a pair of mute swans flew past, their necks outstretched. Watching them drop into the river, she felt as if their bodies, once seemingly weightless, were suddenly too heavy to be held by the air. They circled, touching beak to beak, then turned and swam into the flow of the water. She walked along the towpath and followed them back towards the town.

As the days passed, it became easier not to leave the flat. She stopped going to the gym, stopped her late night swim sessions at the lido, and her weekly drinks with the girls. In the evenings, her voicemail buzzed constantly with friends wanting to catch up, an invite for supper, drinks. Her brother called, his voice loud above the background noise of a pub. 'Hi Ruthie, how are you? I'll pop in later in the week, usual time. Let me know if it's a problem. We must sort out your fortieth.'

She listened to them all, then sent brief text messages saying she was busy at work and would be in touch soon. In a week or two. She wanted to phone the office to plead a flu virus, but that would let people down. There were deadlines to meet, clients to deal with and her staff to consider. It was the end of the tax year, her busiest time; she couldn't just stop, get into bed and hide herself under the covers. She told her secretary that she would work from home. She started to smoke again.

She fell into a strange stasis, sitting at her laptop, not looking at spreadsheets, not making recommendations or writing reports, instead just staring out of the window, her gaze drawn towards the river. Through the walls came the murmur of a television, a raised voice, and all the faint sounds of her neighbours. She thought about the swans swimming seaward with the tide.

One morning, she was surprised to find herself standing by the front door, keys clutched in her hand, her bare feet pushed into shoes and her pyjamas on under her coat.

That same day, around lunchtime, she smoked her last cigarette. How foolish she was to fall into the habit again after so many years. She would stop. But later, her need for nicotine consumed her and forced her out of the flat to the shops. Amongst the shoppers and tourists, she felt insubstantial, as if she were nothing more than her own tattered shadow. Once again, Ruth fled the grey walls of the castle, passed over the bridge, down the steps onto the footpath, and hurried through the fields to the river, all the while hoping the swans would be there.

'Excuse me. Do you think you could help?'

Startled, she swung round to face him. She hadn't been aware of him until he spoke, and now he was so close beside her she felt he had been conjured from the ground. A middle-aged man dressed in jeans and a dark top. He was close enough to smell the musky spice of his aftershave. She stepped away.

'My daughter has gone missing. Please. Would you look at these photos? You may have seen her.'

She should speak, answer him, perhaps commiserate, but couldn't find the words. Behind her, the embankment sloped into the water and, across the floodplain, the bulk of the castle was stark against the hillside. The man held a small, rectangular photograph album. One photo per page. Handbag-size. She remembered her mother had one the same, carrying a much younger Ruth around, trapped in perpetual childhood. He held the album against his chest and flipped it open, its red edges marking strong lines against his black sweatshirt.

She looked at the photograph. A naked woman lay spread-eagled on a bed, a man knelt beside her, his erect penis in his hand. The colours were clear and the detail keen. She could see the orange lampshade, could pick out the shine on the rose satin bedding. The pages turned. Picture replaced picture replaced picture. In each one, the couple were posed ready for sex, on the bed, on the floor, on a sofa. And grinning. Yes, they were grinning. They were looking straight at the lens and grinning for the camera.

Far off on the bypass, a car horn sounded.

Her heart pounded. Her cheeks burned. Breathe, she must breathe. She tried to swallow, but the back of her throat was dry. Shout. She should shout, shove past him, get away. The plastic sleeves covering the photos scratched against each other as he flicked through the album. It wasn't that time stood still, she had simply become immobile within it. The day was stuck, like the stylus on an old record, and she was caught, waiting for someone to lift the needle.

The pages stopped moving. He thrust his hand deep into his trouser pocket. She heard his quick, shallow breaths. She stared at the photograph he held out. The woman was alone, sitting on the edge of an armchair, her breasts, full and round, the nipples, dark jewels against her pale skin. Ruth was captivated. She wanted to reach out and touch the smoothness of the woman's breasts. To see if they were perfect. The album closed with a slap and he slipped it inside his jacket. She raised her head. He was smiling at her. His eyes were kind.

'Thank you for looking,' he said, as he stepped down from the embankment and walked away along the footpath. When he was a dark, distant shape, she turned to follow the river back into town.

The letter from the hospital arrived. With care, she placed it on the table and smoothed it flat. Although the initial prognosis seemed frightening, she should not feel scared, the doctor had reassured her that time in his surgery. The success rate was high. She must not think she was alone.

'There are people to help you through this, Ruth,' he said. When he patted her on the arm, his hand was heavy against her bones. 'And remember, we don't know for sure. At the moment.'

Easy to say, she'd thought. And, as she stood in her living room, she realised she should have asked the doctor why there was no pain at the moment. She should have explained that was the reason she hadn't seen him earlier. But what she should have done no longer mattered.

She decided to tell her brother. Yet, before he was due, she folded the letter back into the envelope and hid it at the bottom of her handbag, along with her cigarettes and lighter. When he arrived, she uncorked a bottle of her favourite red wine and bickered gently with him about what food to order from the Indian takeaway on the corner. They ate, one at each end of the sofa, plates balanced on their knees. She listened while he talked of his work, of ending his current relationship and of a holiday he might book.

'You're quiet,' he remarked, as he mopped round his plate with a piece of naan bread.

'Just tired,' she said, and smiled, nodding her head at the table where her laptop sat surrounded by files.

After he left, she cleared away, stacked the dishwasher, threw the tinfoil containers into a bin liner and rinsed the glasses. The living room was stale with the smell of onions and spices, so she opened the window. She wished she had drunk more wine, wished she had asked her brother to stay, wished he would come back so they could sit up all night and talk. She wanted to call him. Instead, she lit a cigarette and carried a chair to the open window. Sounds floated up from the street, the click of heels on the pavement, snatched words, laughter and the ring of a mobile. With her feet resting on the window sill, she watched her cigarette smoke curl into the darkness.

That night, she began to dream of the man. He had his back to her. She needed to see his face. It was important. She had questions to ask him. In the dream, she tried to recall his features, comparing him to the other men in her life. Did he look like her brother, her father, the doctor, work colleagues, old lovers? She was crying. It was as if the details of his face had fallen from her memory. She reached out and touched his shoulder.

'Please turn around,' she said. She could see her hand resting against the black fabric of his sweatshirt.

She was jolted awake by his voice calling to her.

'Excuse me. Do you think you could help?'

A fingertip brushed her ribcage and, as she jerked away, she felt a trickle of sweat running between her breasts. The glow from the street lights crept around the edges of the curtains, outlining the furniture. Her wardrobe, the chest of drawers in the chimney alcove and her grandma's chair, each piece loomed large in the gloom, as if it had stepped away from the walls and closer to her. Before she could turn on the bedside lamp, images from the photographs spooled in front of her eyes. One after another, they juddered like the snatch of pictures in a home movie.

There was his voice, full of confidence. 'Make sure you look properly.'

Come morning, as she lay in her stale bedding, a rancid stickiness on her skin, she was surprised to find she was alone. With her legs drawn up and her arms clamped around her breasts, she felt older than she believed it was possible to feel.

The dreams began to seep into her daytime thoughts. She started to wonder about the people in the photographs. Who were they? Did they have children? Where did they live? Was this their main job? Taking off their clothes, sliding their bodies across each other, was it how they paid the bills? Paid for food? She thought about the woman's breasts. They were flawless. In her mind's eye, she pictured the woman easing her fingers into the firmness of those perfect breasts. She imagined how the woman felt as the flesh surrendered to her touch, as she, this nameless, unknown woman, felt for an invisible, painless lump.

Always a soft voice telling her, 'Don't be scared.' It sounded like the doctor. It could have been the man.

She thought of other hands, strong and capable, with wiry dark hairs on the back of the thumb, the fingers prodding and probing her body, bruising her. She looked at her own hands, wrapped around a coffee mug. The skin was creased, the veins raised and blue. She could not think that these hands belonged to her.

On the day of her operation, she was up at dawn. She packed a bag and left it in the hallway. Leaving her pyjamas on the floor, she stood naked, feeling the warmth of her breasts in her cupped hands. She dressed in loose clothes, comforted by the familiar soft cotton of her t-shirt, close against her skin.

Outside, the early morning air was fresh and clean. She put the bag on the passenger seat of her car, locked the door, and began to walk, striding along, feeling the hard pavement through the soles of her shoes. The town was quiet. It felt peaceful as it waited for the hustle of the delivery lorries. On the crest of the bridge, she paused and rested her arms on the parapet, her breasts pressed tight against the smooth stone.

The Arun was high. The undertow would be strong, grasping at the banks, dragging debris far upstream. She scratched her nails into the mortar and a scrap of yellow lichen fell free, spiralling down to the water. She could see the empty towpath cutting through the flood plain and curving away from the town. The breeze brought the whistle of the train, the rumble of traffic, the bark of a dog and the throb of beating wings. She lifted her face to the wind and saw the swans. Eight of them, necks outstretched, dashes of white against the blue sky, flying towards the river. She glanced down at her watch. It was time to go.

To the Sea

The Stone Marker

INSTEAD OF CUTTING, he circles the stone. When he worked the piece yesterday, some of the hollows had deepened and the first signs had emerged in a series of gentle curves. He looks for the possibilities, an arm, the arc of a backbone or the fan of a wing. He runs his hands across the surface, hoping he can understand the rhythms from the grain. It's time to open up the piece, and he's not sure what to keep and what to discard. This uncertainty fills him with fear.

Set at the bottom of the garden, sitting on the grass next to his wooden studio, the rocky mass looks incongruous, at odds with the surroundings in a way he hadn't expected. Yet, a few months ago at the quarry, he'd studied the block from all angles for faults, trying to judge its character, looking for a piece that would yield to the chisel and be pleasing to sculpt. He felt excited, overwhelmed by choice. So often in the past he'd favoured limestone, he understood it, knew it was trustworthy, knew it carved well and liked the way it cut. He'd been pleased with his choice. But, looking at the bone-white bulk hunched on a pallet like a silent visitor, he feels he may have been unwise. Gusts of wind lift the canvas roof of his makeshift shelter, the noise reminding him of the boom of waves against distant cliffs.

It's still wintry this early in the morning, but the March sun hints at warmth to come later in the day and the slight frosting on the lawn will disappear in an hour or two. Earlier, he stopped to pick some of the daffodils edging the path, hoping the yellow would look cheerful if he popped them in jugs around the cottage. When he snapped the stalks, the sap smelt green and new. It left a gummy film across his fingers that he wiped on the leg of his jeans. He was disappointed, not realising how short the stems were this year, their growth stunted by the wet, cold ground. His haul was meagre, a paltry apology instead of a colourful peace offering.

After resting the flowers on top of the chicken house, he opened the door and released the birds into the run. The reek of fresh droppings hung in the air as he gathered six warm brown eggs from the nesting box. He wiped off scraps of straw, manure and feathers, and rolled each one in his palm before placing it into a plastic bowl. He scattered corn and a few crusts of bread, pausing to watch the hens push and peck for the best scraps.

Indoors, he put the basin of eggs on the draining board. Amongst the muddle of their kitchen, the kettle was cold and the radio silent. Dirty china littered the worktop, leaving a faint trace of last night's fish pie and cauliflower. He would be starting work later than he wanted, yet he stacked the dishwasher, filled the log baskets in the sitting room and arranged his handful of flowers in a glass, placing it next to the laptop on the clean, pine table. Then, snatching up his studio keys from the fruit bowl on the dresser, he left.

By habit, he'd stopped at the place where the path curves behind the tall hawthorn hedge and glanced back at the cottage. The light was catching the windows, and the red brick of the walls and grey slate roof looked sturdy against the backdrop of a blue sky. When he looked up at the spare bedroom, the curtains were still closed.

He must concentrate. He lines up the point chisel and, with the familiar heft of the hammer in his hand, begins to bite grooves and ridges across the stone. He guesses that Annie has dressed, picturing her in the oversized red jumper and black leggings she has taken to wearing. Chips of limestone hit the damp earth without a sound. She'd stayed upstairs again, waiting for him to leave, no doubt sitting on the chair in the alcove, listening for the click of the Yale as he closed the door. He should have taken coffee up to her, or at the very least called out, 'Goodbye.' He can't remember ever leaving her without a word, yet these last couple of weeks it's been the easiest thing to do. Sometimes silence is better for both of them.

As he works the stone, he remembers how, in their twenties, they hadn't worried about anything. He finished art school, worked part-time in a pub and set up his studio. Annie took any job she could find, admin, receptionist, dog walker, she never cared. All that mattered was coming home to work on her novels. They were lucky, their reputations grew. Annie's stories, woven through with myths and legends, gathered a following and, although they never made a fortune, her books had begun to sell. Alongside some teaching, commissions for his stone markers began to trickle in too. Rob Willis, Sculptor. He became known for producing forms for public spaces, works that carried a sense of their surroundings, a sense of place. Over the years, his pieces became rooted in the landscape, each softening beneath the elements into a flaking, lichened grey.

He turns the chisel and cuts back over the same area, cross-hatching the surface. It seems as if he can recall every word they spoke last night, hearing his own voice so loudly it stifles the peck of the blade against the stone. What is it with Annie? At their age they have everything they want. Christ, they can do anything they feel like. Aren't they always busy? Full lives, that's what they have. She'd accused him of over-reacting, when anyone would agree he's the one being sensible. As he said, he was thinking it through and considering more than just himself. Unlike her.

He wishes he hadn't shouted last night, wishes he hadn't smashed his fist onto the worktop, and wishes he hadn't accused her of being bloody selfish. Most of all, he wishes those last words had stayed unspoken. When he stops to reposition, he realises he has buried the edge of the chisel and bruised the stone. A silly mistake, careless, and one he's always warning his students about. He sits back on his heels. It's warm and he is sheltered by the bulk of the sculpture. Fat pigeons call from the studio roof. Close by, a car door slams followed by the thump of a diesel engine as the vehicle drives down the lane. He's glad. It will do Annie good to get out for a while.

This evening, he will not raise his voice. Instead, he'll try again to explain how he feels. How he was sure she had always felt the same. He lifts his face towards the sun. Yes, he'll tell her he thought they were all right as they were. He flexes his shoulders and selects a flat chisel. Once more, the edge moves across the surface. He'll have to carve deeper to remove the blemish and, using gentle taps, he begins to repair the damage.

As he packs his tools away and locks the studio, he runs through what he'll say, testing each sentence, trying to guess her reply. He checks the chickens on his way past, shutting them into the safety of the nest box for the night. Annie's car is not on the drive next to the cottage, and his battered red van stands alone on the gravel. He fishes his house keys out of his pocket and unlocks the back door.

He is greeted by a settled stillness, a heavy silence that permeates the house. When he looks around the room, he sees her handbag is missing, her duffel coat is not on the hook and the laptop has gone. In the study, her desk is tidy, the rubbish bin empty and her books are stacked neatly on the shelves. Upstairs, her dressing gown is not hanging behind the bathroom door and he can't see her pyjamas. He checks both bedrooms. She left hours ago. He's cheated by her absence. On the table, the daffodil buds are beginning to unfurl, their welcome is out of place in the lingering emptiness. He reaches for the small envelope left propped against the makeshift vase.

The gravity of what she's telling him is so obvious that he looks away and lets the letter fall onto the table. She promises not to take risks. She'll be looked after, she says. They'll be looked after. Please, Rob, don't worry. And don't call her or text, that way they can't argue. She can't bear the arguments.

Through the window, the wind stirs the bare branches of the willow against the backdrop of evening light. He stays where he is, sitting at the table, head in his hands, listening to the tick of the clock, the hum of the fridge and the intermittent creak of the water pipes. Is she really devastated that he is not happy? Doesn't she really know how to talk to him anymore? Are these things true? We can't live like this, she says. It's not doing us any good.

He should eat and, standing, finds his joints stiff and limbs cramped. He puts two slices of wholemeal under the grill, takes the butter dish from the fridge and places it on the worktop, tracing his finger down the crack in the lid. They should get a new dish. Go out together and choose one. The scent of warm toast fills the kitchen, and he takes it from the grill and leaves it, unbuttered, on the plate.

It's still dark when he folds the letter back into the envelope. The room is cold. Although it's too early for the heating to come on, he flicks the switch and stands, arms folded, leaning against the radiator, waiting for the warmth to come through. He's bone weary. His students are due at the studio tomorrow to look at the stone, and he must prepare for them. His hands shake when he shaves, seeing his father's face looking back out of the mirror, as if he, Rob, has aged overnight. Dressed in a washed-out grey sweatshirt and old jeans, he makes coffee. Waiting for the kettle, he takes up the envelope and props it back against the glass of daffodils.

The cottage is empty without Annie, so he drinks his coffee standing in the garden, waiting for the sun to rise. Why had he shouted? Is she right? How can they discuss things when he loses his temper? He's not really cross with her, surely she understands that. Close by, from high in a holly bush, the insistent early morning song of a blackbird interrupts his thoughts. His neighbour's cat steals through the shrubs along the boundary, and he spots the streak of ginger fur against the gunmetal flint of the garden wall.

Back in the kitchen, he calls her mobile and, with the phone hard against his ear, listens to her voice saying she can't answer right now. He hangs up.

At the studio, he closes his eyes and runs his hands across the surface of the stone, feeling the arcs and dips he has cut over the previous days, hoping this time he can see something of the form through the tips of his fingers. The piece is an enigma. Unlike his previous work, he did not draw a design directly onto the face of the rock and had no preconceived ideas of any shape at the start. It feels strange, challenging. He calls it his 'mid-life crisis'. All he has is the belief that he'll know this stone marker when it evolves from the block. Yet he's troubled by this sense of stepping into the unknown, and working on the sculpture remains unrealistic whilst his vision for the piece is out of reach. Tomorrow, the students will arrive and there is nothing in the stone to show them. He didn't think when choosing the limestone that this would be a problem. He reaches for a hammer and begins to work, letting the ringing taps of the chisel block out the uproar in his head.

The evening is already darkening when he finishes work. At the cottage, he leaves the curtains open and lies on their bed in his clothes. The muscles in his shoulders ache and he needs to eat. With his face turned into the pillow, he catches a trace of perfume. Annie. All that matters is their life together, the Saturday night curries at their local, sitting on the sofa watching an old film with a bowl of popcorn between them, plays at the theatre and, more than anything else, their plans for the future.

He reaches for the silver-framed photo on top of the bedside cabinet, the one he'd taken fifteen years ago on a trip to California. Annie, aged thirty, perched cross-legged on a bench, her dark hair twisted high on her head, exposing the tender sweep of her neck. His Annie, eating ice cream on the boardwalk at Monterey, the crash of Pacific waves for company. How she loved it there. How she'd wanted to stay. She was sure she could write wonderful stories in this place and he would carve huge, polished stones. All she wanted was to set up there. It would be easy to do, she told him. Let's stay until we're forty. Better still, we could stay forever and grow old here. No chance, the ground is too flat, he joked. I am an artist and I need height. I need mountains, he cried, jumping up and standing on the seat. Laughing, she had grabbed his legs and, overbalanced, he fell onto the sand.

For him, it was all about stone. He was drawn inland, enthralled by the colours of the rocks and the vast isolation of the wilderness. It was all about the ancient sequoias and the harsh granite splendour of the Sierra Nevada. There was a moment when he had considered staying and setting up his own workshop, but it was only that, a moment. In truth, staying there had been Annie's dream.

He turns towards the window and watches the first star appear in a cloudless night sky below the thin crescent of the moon. It's true, exactly as Annie has written. They've waited a long time. It's easy to see why Annie is excited. He understands. After all, this is something they've always wanted. Yet, as the years passed, he thought they'd both come to believe it would never happen. Yes, he's frightened. Who wouldn't be? Perhaps, underneath it all, Annie may be a little bit scared as well. He hopes not. Soon, the days will lengthen and the stone will move on to its new home. He feels light-headed, nauseous, and when he gets up in search of food, he leaves a dusty imprint on the quilt.

He opens cupboards at random, grabbing a bowl and some soup. He turns the radio on, but the talking is intrusive and the laughter of a panel show irritates him. He turns it off again. The letter is still on the table with 'Rob' written in her large untidy scrawl across the front. His stomach growls and, checking his wallet for cash, he considers going to the pub for a meal or getting fish and chips. At last, he breaks two eggs into a saucepan, whisks in milk, adds butter and stirs them as they scramble. They simply need space, him and Annie, time alone to get used to everything. She loves him. And she's only gone to her mum's, she'll be home soon. Annie will be back for their first scan. He eats the eggs, stacks his crockery in the dishwasher and, standing in the middle of the kitchen, reads the letter again.

His students arrive in a series of youthful shouts and good-humoured jokes. They're keen to see the piece again and quick to make visual judgements, a lion's head, an eagle, the arc of a leaping salmon. Each suggestion seems to him childish, more outlandish than the last, and their lack of empathy for the work exhausts him. To cover his impatience, he explains how the rock was formed, how a nucleus made from a fragment of shell rolled across the sea floor, gathering calcite and growing in size. Over time, countless billions of these egg-stones became cemented together and gradually the limestone beds took shape. He speaks of the patches of chert, the fossils, and all the imperfections that were formed millions of years ago in the ocean bed ooze of warm, shallow seas.

He asks them to think about the compliant nature of the stone, of undercutting, of texture, explaining ways of bringing the stone to life, pointing out features in the block. Grabbing a flat chisel, he starts to smooth across yesterday's carving, removing the ridges. Little by little, he is soothed by the cadence of his work, and with swift movements he cleans out the concave cuts.

After the students have gone, he gathers up his tools and sweeps around the cutting area using a small brush, collecting all the fragments from the pallet and the larger pieces from the grass. When he is satisfied, he stands back and takes stock of the day's work. For the first time he can see that the mark of the chisel has started to unite the surface and, at long last, it begins to read as one. To one side, he can make out the soft shape of a head in profile, leading down to the gentle sweep of a swollen breast and, emerging from the stone, the rising crescent of a belly.

As he makes his way back to the cottage, he hears the growl of a diesel engine in the lane. He hurries through the chilly dusk. The evening smells of wet leaves and his neighbour's wood smoke. In the flower beds, clusters of purple and white hellebores push up between the autumn-pruned stems of the rose bushes, their delicate flowers translucent against their strong evergreen leaves.

Rock Islands

TO THE EAST, the bulk of the rock islands stretch across Elmer Sands. At a distance, they are graceful, a series of crescents echoing the bow of the coastline. One year, woken in the night by the booms carried on the still air, I listened as boulders were laid on the beach. Tucked in my narrow bed at our rented cottage, it felt as if the ground trembled beneath the weight of the stones as they were manoeuvred into place. Each day, at low tide, I stood on the path, guessing which rocks were new, watching as the islands were pushed into shape. At the end of the holiday, I wanted to stay. That was twenty-eight years ago, and I'd been an angry ten year old who told her parents that she wished this was their home, that she wanted to be here, by the sea, while the islands gradually rose from the sand.

I arrive in the evening, turning into Blake's Road and driving towards the seafront, hoping for a parking space. It all looks much the same. Through the open window comes a familiar screeching of gulls and the thud of balls against the hard surface of the tennis courts. I park, step onto the pavement, tug my hair free from its ponytail and ease the kinks from my shoulders. My shirt is wrinkled from the seatbelt and I have to pluck at the loose material to shake the creases free. Across the picnic area, the pebbles give way to shingle, then sand and, far out beyond the breakwaters, the flat, green sea.

On the horizon, a ship appears motionless, trapped between sea and sky. I'm not sure, but I think it could be a dredger from Littlehampton clearing the shingle from the mouth of the River Arun. One holiday, standing in the rain on the quayside, Dad explained how a great clawed bucket is lowered from the boat. As we watched the tug heading off towards Shoreham with its load, he told me the bucket went down through the water to scoop up the seabed. Raindrops pattered onto our umbrella and his hand was a gentle pressure on my shoulder.

The air is leaden. It has lost the fresh, salt tang of the open water under scents of frying chips and sun-baked seaweed. I should eat sometime soon but my stomach heaves and all I can taste is bile burning the back of my throat. On the passenger seat, my mobile buzzes and I reach in to grab it. It won't be work, that's definite. Not after I called them earlier claiming a migraine. The bank will have to manage without me for a couple of days. I glance at the screen and see the caller is James. I lean against the warm metal door and shut my eyes for a few seconds. Light flickers behind my closed eyelids then fades until there is no more than sepia space. Without reading the message, I turn the mobile off, drop it into my bag and lock the car.

A group of children crowd around the ice cream kiosk. Their voices are high and their laughter irritates me. Listening to them confuses me for a moment. Edging through, I concentrate on the advertising slogans on the wall above their heads. Twister. Fab. Feast. Strange, these are the same lollies I remember from my childhood. The colours on the metal sign are sharp and slick in the evening sunlight.

Outside the café, the tables are full. Two young girls hurry about delivering food, their legs long and tanned beneath short, black skirts. They move with grace amongst the diners, carrying plates and clearing china, bobbing and bending as quickly as sandpipers teetering along the shore. When I was growing up, we rented a cottage on this stretch of coast every spring, and in the mornings, after breakfast, we hurried around the corner, passing the café and the sailing club, to open up our beach hut. I helped Mum and Dad repair the winter's damage, rubbing down flaking woodwork, resealing the felt roof and clearing silver-fish from empty cupboards. Back in the cottage, when Dad kissed me goodnight, his hair had tickled the smell of gloss paint across my cheek. On

Easter Sunday, we would stop work for a while, break open our eggs and eat them with our morning tea, the melting chocolate, rich and viscous in my mouth.

School friends boasted of fortnights in Spain and France, but I never felt envious. To me, all our work at the beach hut carried a promise of the summer yet to come. Six weeks of shrimp nets and lilos, ice lollies and chips. I looked forward to games of football and cricket on the beach, barbecues on the greensward, and to days spent with children who, like me, returned each year. Released every morning from the holiday lets, we flocked together to play, bonded by our possession of the small wooden buildings.

I loved our beach hut. It was steadfast, like the best type of friend, the kind I read about in books. A friend I wanted to have adventures with. It was whipped by the wind, scorched by the sun and buffeted through the winter by storms. To me, it defied all weathers. It was my castle on a cliff. I loved the heavy boules set that remained through the year and the old plastic tennis rackets tucked in a box in the corner of the hut. There were tins of biscuits, bags of crisps and squash drunk from my holiday mug. Thick, white china dotted with seabirds, and my name, Emma, written in red around the rim. But most of all, I loved the getting here. I loved being packed into the back of the car with folding picnic chairs and the camping stove, and I always held my breath as we drove up onto the top of the Downs. This was the start of the holiday, and I was waiting for the right moment to shout, 'there it is'. Even though my first glimpse of the sea was no more than a thin ribbon of silver glistening in the distance.

The girls have cleared the table nearest me. It would be nice to sit for a while, perhaps order a drink. Instead, I keep on walking. My parents no longer paint the hut themselves and the colour they've chosen comes as a surprise. The yellow is brash and false, the hut too polished and perfect. It's glossy, like the picture postcards I sent to my friends. I must keep this in mind when I come to decorate the spare bedroom. No matter what happens, I'm sure it will be better to emulsion the walls a soft, matt white. Maybe I'll paint a frieze of beach huts and deckchairs. Or lighthouses and boats. Then, from the ceiling, I could hang a mobile and string it with gulls made of felt.

I undo the padlocks, let down the deck and open the door. The keys are warm in my hand, as if they hold an echo of the summer. Mum and Dad still use the keyring I won at the fair. After twenty-five years of use, it's no wonder the little red boat is scuffed and the clasp is squashed out of shape. Inside, the hut looks the same, with a neat pile of blankets and old towels folded in one corner, and the picnic chairs and sun beds stacked against a wall. They've bought new cushions; the covers, with their riot of overblown roses, looking out of place in this world of sea and sand.

With a cushion wedged into the small of my back, I settle down on the deck, legs stretched out in front and shoulders pressed against the warm woodwork. Unbidden, James invades my thoughts. Clean-shaven, a love of crisp white shirts and silk ties, the glint of gold cufflinks placed carefully, side by side, on the glass top of my dressing table. This is James. And the book I ordered for him left open, its spine broken, abandoned on the floor by the bed. This too is James.

On weekdays, I usually join him for supper. We eat early in small restaurants or bistros, then, holding hands in the back of a taxi, are driven through the streets to my flat. He tells me the stories of his successes, the deals he's closed and the clients he's met.

In bed, he tells me how together I am. My Miss Independent, he murmurs, stroking my hair. As often as we can, we swim at the gym. James, head down, feet kicking, arms slicing through the water, his body racing through lap after lap of a fierce front crawl. While I like to drift with a quiet breaststroke, bobbing along in his wake.

I think the best thing is to catch sight of him off guard. To see his profile replicated in the mirrors of the wardrobe, or watch for his reflection in a shop window as he hurries down the street to meet me. There is something about the beak of his nose and the jut of his chin. These snatched images are my luxury. I store them up. He calls himself my older man. Older and wiser, Poppet, he jokes, holding me close for a kiss. On Fridays, he always makes sure to have a shower before he catches the last train home.

And when he's gone, leaving me in my dressing gown to curl up on the sofa and look back over our week, that's when I think about all the stolen glimpses.

Saturdays and Sundays, I like to visit art galleries and museums. Sometimes I shop at Borough Market for artisan bread and cheese. There's a café near the market, by the ruins of Winchester Palace, and I sit in the courtyard, coffee on the table, with the grey stone of the one remaining wall towering above me. And there are trips to the cinema and meals with friends. It's funny, we can chat about most things me and my friends, work or politics, books. All the normal things. But when it comes to talking about relationships, well, then I don't say much, and I never mention James. If the weather's fine, I'm happy sitting on my balcony with a glass of wine, catching up on my reading. Back in the spring, I planted up the window boxes. The geraniums are growing thick and strong, the flower buds tight and full, and it doesn't bother me that the crimson petals of the plants are at odds with the dull, brown brick of the building.

James would hate to see me look like this. You are a sight, he'd say, his nostrils flaring. Yet here I am with crumpled clothes and messy hair, sitting by the beach hut, gazing out at the sea. Going over it all in my mind, there are things in our relationship I am certain I'll never forget. Like how it was the night I told him. How his cheeks burned with anger, two red patches flaming across his face. How he turned away, his fists clenched and his back rigid, staring out through the window into the night. In the end, he spoke. What the hell are you thinking? I mean, in god's name, are you really that damn stupid? Jesus Christ, what a bloody mess. His voice sounded cold and flat against the glass.

One by one, the huts close for the night. Children run up the greensward carrying plastic buckets filled with pebbles, shells and seaweed. Families regroup ready to leave, and all the detritus of a day at the beach is folded, shaken and packed away. The light is dimming when the last door closes, the last deck is lifted and the padlocks all snapped into place. Like the row of castles I once imagined they were, their portcullises are shut and their drawbridges are raised. My back is stiff when I bend to gather up the cushion.

I should leave, yet I fill the kettle at the standpipe and sit inside the beach hut, waiting for the sun to set.

Through the open door, I watch the incoming tide, the waves spitting across the shingle, as if fighting the pull of the rising moon. Thank goodness my stomach has settled at last. I snack on crisps and plain biscuits and lie on the bench, covering myself with a rug. My arms and legs feel weary, my breasts tender, and my body, hot and flushed. I'm remembering a little girl, racing to the sea and back, collecting water in her two plastic buckets. Over and over, she runs, not stopping, until the moat around her sandcastle is overflowing. The child writes *EMMA* in purple crayoned capitals on a flag and sets it into the highest turret. The paper whips and snaps as it catches the breeze.

❧

I sleep fitfully and wake early. For a moment, I lie on my back, hands resting on the slight rise of my stomach. Next door to the café, in the sailing club, some boats are hauled up, high and dry on the concrete with the wind singing through their masts and ropes.

I boil water on the camping stove, shove my phone in my pocket and carry my coffee outside into the salty air. My footsteps are silent on the grass. Steam rises up from the mug and I catch a bitter scent. A rush of saliva floods my mouth. I sit on my favourite bench with my bare feet resting on the low wall. My toenails are short and neat, the polish pearlescent. Once, James told me I had peasant's feet. Broad and flat, he said, with a grin.

Overnight, the tide has turned and again the distant sea is flat and calm, the water's edge blurring against the sand. The beach is littered with lumps of chalk left behind by the ebbing waves.

As a child, I thought these rocks had fallen from the moon as it journeyed across the oceans. All through the holidays, I carried a small, white piece tucked safe in the pocket of my jeans.

Two nuns from the convent school cycle along the promenade. As they peddle, their veils stream out into the wind like jib sails and their habits billow around their knees above thick, dark tights and old-fashioned shoes. They smile – *Good Morning* – as they pass. I'm not sure if the Catholic hotel is still on the corner. It always fascinated me, with its black and white woodwork on the gable ends and windows, like winking eyes, set high under the curve of the roof. Often, there were nuns sitting on the balcony enjoying the sun. Queuing at the kiosk, I always hoped I would turn, ice lolly in hand, to find one of the sisters standing in line behind me, waiting for her turn to buy an ice cream.

I switch on the phone; messages flash and buzz. Voicemails from James. He needs to see me. He's sorry if he sounded angry, but surely I can see he's right. He knows this is something neither of us wants. We must talk sensibly. He admits he was surprised, no, shocked, but as he said at the time, there is a way out. Privately, he means. He'll sort it. A voicemail from Mum. She wonders if I'll be spending my birthday with them, but will understand if I've made other plans. A text. James again. Why are you doing this to me? Just call back.

I'm not sure when the tide will turn, so I check the timetable on my phone. I need to leave now. I throw the remains of the coffee on the ground. It pools before disappearing into the grass. There is a small brass plaque on the bench and, before leaving, I run my hand across the words, *In Loving Memory of Gladys and Lionel.* My fingertips glide across the curves and lines of the inscription etched into the metal and, although I don't know these people, it would be nice to have met them.

The shallow sea is warm and, as I walk, tiny fish dart over my feet. Up ahead, water pours from the storm drain, cutting a stream in the sand. Beyond the pebbles, near the promenade, I can make out the shapes of wind-bent shrubs pushing up from the ground. Here the concrete stops, surrendering to the mud and wild grass of the footpath. From the water's edge, there are no signs of the villas and holiday lets that line this stretch of coast, yet they are there, tucked behind rendered walls and scrubby pine windbreaks, their balconies no doubt cluttered with tables and chairs. I keep going, leaving the bustle of the café and kiosk, the beach huts and sailing club, following the soft sweep of the coast as it curves around Middleton Point towards the islands.

The ebb tide is low, the water far from the land. Sunlight glistens across every surface. The beach stretches away, inviting me to carry on. There's a slight give in the sand and I begin to stride out, straightening my back and swinging my arms with each pace. After a while, the muscles in my calves begin to ache. There's no doubt about it, I'll hurt tomorrow, but that doesn't seem to matter.

When I reach the rock islands, the sand gives way under my feet, each step revealing a hidden layer of black mud, the residue of rotted seaweed. It's hard to keep my balance here, in the shade of these exposed sea defences. I'm tired but can't see anywhere to rest. Coarse-shelled barnacles cover the islands, clinging for their lives to the boulders. They are all over the surface, packed in tight across the face of the stone, waiting for the return of the waves.

As my friends have pointed out, there is no 'Emma and James'. As a couple, we've made no plans for the future. We have no history. In our time together, those brief snatched hours between work and home, we've spoken only of the present. I've never told James about the holidays at the beach hut, never mentioned the rock islands or the summers when I watched as the tide went out and the islands emerged from the sea. I've never spoken of how, on the very first morning of the holidays, when I tugged the winter-warped door of the hut open, I had to close my eyes against the flecks of loose paint as they fell, coarse as windblown sand, against my cheeks.

And while I've never visited his company flat and know very little about his life in the country, I've always known about the photograph he keeps in his wallet. He's there, in the picture, tall and strong with his arm draped across the shoulders of a pretty woman, and flanked by two laughing boys, both nearly as tall as their father. I shiver. It's chilly standing here in the shadows.

Waves are moving rapidly up the sand. I need to hurry; in a couple of hours all the beach will be gone and the waves will swirl around the base of the islands, the water rising up until the rocks disappear beneath the sea. I'm about to walk back along the shore when there is a stirring inside me. With my hands against the curve of my belly, I can feel a flutter deep in my core.

Back at the beach huts, families have set up camp for the day. Windbreaks have been hammered into the ground and sun loungers opened. Some children are playing with a yellow frisbee, throwing it high into the air, a disc of sunshine spinning in the breeze. Maybe later I will speak to James. I'll have to, but there's no rush. Right now there's a new day's aroma of chips and I am hungry. I unlock the hut, grab my bag and make my way towards the café. As I wait for my food, I turn my phone on. Ignoring James's messages, I call Mum and Dad. I'll definitely be spending my birthday with them. Will they be in later if I pop in with the key? Yes, dinner would be great, thanks. I sip my coffee.

Setting my bag on the ground, I spot a small, white stone by my feet. Perfectly ovate, its surface has been shaped and smoothed by the movement of a million tides. I pick up the chalk and hold it safe in my hand. Down at the water's edge, a woman stands with a baby in her arms. She swoops the child down towards the waves, and up again. Her laughter is carried towards the café on the breeze. The water splashes around them, the drops catching in the light.

Acknowledgements

For my family and friends, whose continual support is invaluable. My heartfelt thanks also goes to the Department of English and Creative Writing at the University of Chichester: Alison MacLeod, Stephen Mollett, Stephanie Norgate, Karen Stevens and Dave Swann. And to Jess de Mellow, who started this adventure.

To those who read the early drafts: Hannah Radcliffe, Annabel Mackenzie, Dave Frankel and Morgaine Davidson. With special thanks to Jez Noond, who helped me to shape the stories into a collection.

I would also like to thank the following prizes and publications, which gave me the encouragement to keep writing. 'Magpie' was shortlisted for the Bristol Short Story Prize 2015 and included in its anthology *The Bristol Short Story Prize Volume 8 2015*. 'The Beekeeper's Daughters' was shortlisted for the Willesden Herald Short Story Award 2014 and included in its anthology *Willesden Herald New Short Stories 8*. 'Tilting at Windmills' was Seren Books' story of the month in May 2017. 'The Broom Maker' was shortlisted for the Storgy Short Story Award 2015. 'Undercurrents' was runner up in the Willesden Herald Short Story Award 2016 and included in its anthology *Willesden Herald New Short Stories 9*. 'Rock Islands' was highly commended in the Ink Tears Short Story Award 2015.

And my thanks to Jamie McGarry and Jo Haywood at Valley Press for making this happen.

Milton Keynes UK
Ingram Content Group UK Ltd.
UKHW042235120524
442564UK00001B/22

9 781912 436224